Hunt the Man Down

Center Point
Large Print

Also by William Heuman and available from Center Point Large Print:

Guns at Broken Bow
On to Santa Fe
Then Came Mulvane
Gunhand from Texas
Bullets for Mulvane
Roll the Wagons

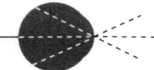

**This Large Print Book carries the
Seal of Approval of N.A.V.H.**

Hunt the Man Down

William Heuman

CENTER POINT LARGE PRINT
THORNDIKE, MAINE

This Center Point Large Print edition
is published in the year 2024 by arrangement with
Golden West Inc.

Copyright © 1951 by Fawcett Publications, Inc.

All rights reserved.

Originally published in the US by
Fawcett Publications, Inc.

The text of this Large Print edition is unabridged.
In other aspects, this book may vary
from the original edition.
Printed in the United States of America
on permanent paper sourced using
environmentally responsible foresting methods.
Set in 16-point Times New Roman type.

ISBN 979-8-89164-075-7 (hardcover)
ISBN 979-8-89164-079-5 (paperback)

The Library of Congress has cataloged this record
under Library of Congress Control Number: 2023950449

Chapter One

The way Cass Lorimer found the man was strange indeed. He spotted the horse first—a dapple gray, saddled, the reins trailing, standing in a little hollow about a dozen yards off the stage road which led to Red Rock. He would have passed the animal by, thinking it was no concern of his that a lone rider had pulled off the road for a moment, but he was attracted by the peculiar behavior of the gray.

The horse snorted several times, and then stamped the ground nervously. Cass turned his own buckskin off the road and down into the hollow, following the tracks made by the gray, and he noticed with interest that the tracks were not too fresh. He figured that they'd been made that morning, and it was now about two o'clock in the afternoon. Why a rider would turn off the stage road at this desolate spot, and then leave his horse, saddled and bridled, for five or six hours at least, was a puzzle.

Frowning, Cass dismounted stiffly, staring toward the stand of pine about thirty yards distant. This was rather barren country, cattle country, with here and there short stretches of timber.

The gray horse edged away as Cass came up,

and then he saw the bootprints leading away toward the timber. He noticed the way the heels of the boots dug deeply into the soft loam, and then the way they weaved from side to side. He thought at first that perhaps the man was wounded, but there was no blood, and then he saw something gleaming in the hot sun a few yards off the trail left by this stranger.

Stepping over, Cass picked it up, and the glass was hot from the sun. It was a whisky bottle, empty. He threw it aside again, a cold smile on his face, understanding the reason for this weaving path up toward the stand of pine. The rider of the dapple gray was asleep in the shade there, so drunk that he'd left his mount in the hot sun for half a day.

Tempted to turn back and forget the whole incident, Cass thought of the gray standing all through the heat of the day while its drunken owner slept in the shade. He kept on then for the stand of timber, following those weaving steps. He wasn't quite prepared for what he found.

The man sat on the fallen trunk of a tree, leaning back against another tree, his head hanging to one side. He was a thin-faced man, bony and with black hair, a stubble of dark whiskers on his face, indicating that he had not shaved that day and possibly the previous day as well. He had a wedge of a chin, a thin, hooked nose and thin lips—slack in death now. The gun, a Navy

Colt .45, hung limp in his right hand. He had blown his brains out.

There were flies buzzing around the powder-blackened hole in his right temple. He'd been dead for quite some time. His black, flat-crowned hat lay on the ground where it had fallen. He wore a black coat and vest, and a rather soiled white shirt. A gold watch chain dangled from the vest pocket.

Cass Lorimer noticed his hands—long and thin, and uncalloused, and that could mean something. This man had not been a rider for one of the outfits in this territory. He was not a man who worked with his hands for a living. A gambling man would have hands like that, or another type of man—the man who lived by the gun.

The black coat was opened, and Cass could see the holster inside—black, smooth, soft leather, well oiled. That Navy Colt was not the type of gun a gambler ordinarily would carry. He would have a smaller pocket weapon—possibly a derringer. Cass Lorimer looked at the holster, at the gun and at the man, and wondered.

Maybe half over a drunk, disgusted with himself, fed up with life, his mind confused. Sitting alone here in this quiet grove with the sun streaming down through the branches. Maybe it had been an impulse; maybe he'd been thinking about it for a long time, a worm crawling around inside his head. It hadn't taken long, just the second or two necessary for a man familiar with a six-gun to draw and squeeze gently on the trigger. It had been quick, painless. Then oblivion.

He didn't search the man's body. He'd noticed the saddle bag on the side of the dapple gray, and he went back to the horse. There wasn't too much in the bag—another full bottle of whisky, some tobacco, an old newspaper, and a small, rathered battered, leather-bound Bible.

Cass looked at the Bible curiously. On the flyleaf was inscribed very neatly in a woman's hand, "Ty Kincaid."

The ink was faded, scarcely legible now, and Cass wondered how many years this man Ty Kincaid had carried the book with him, possibly only as a good-luck talisman. His luck, good and bad, had ended forever here under the pines.

Slipping the saddle off the gray, Cass dumped saddle, blanket roll and saddle bag in among the bushes, and gave the gray a slap across the rump. The animal chased out of the hollow. There was plenty of grass and water in this country, and the chances were that it would stay in the vicinity.

Cass didn't go back to the dead man in the grove. Red Rock was still about two hours ride to the north, and the sheriff and the local coroner could take over from there.

Back on the stage road, heading north again, he forgot for some time his own mission in this country, thinking about the dead man in the grove. Remembrance came back to him when he spotted landmarks he'd been told to look for. There was a bluff to the right of the stage road, and then a corduroy road which led up the grade to the left of the road. He turned the buckskin up the corduroy road which led through timber for several hundred yards, and then ended in open grass.

Years before this timber had been cut down, and the corduroy road had been used by the lumber men. The new growth had reached a fairly good height already.

He was to push due west after leaving the corduroy road, until he reached the stream, a pebbly little creek which trickled across a meadow. Following the stream for about a mile, moving north again, he located the homestead—what was left of it.

The house had been little more than a sod shanty, and it had fallen in. A snake slithered out of the dugout as he rode up, disappearing among the rocks. There had been a number of outbuildings and sheds, and the remains of a corral. He noticed that the barn had been burned down, and he saw the charred embers strewn around.

He didn't find the grave; he didn't look for the grave, but he knew where it was—up on the slope beyond the barn. Emily had told him where to find it, but he didn't go there. He sat astride the buckskin horse, a tall man, straight in the saddle, a lean, angular face, high cheekbones. His eyes under the rim of the black, flat-crowned hat were gray, bleak, as he looked at the ruin of this homestead. Trail dust clung to his gray flannel shirt and to his vest; it tinged his black hair under the sombrero.

A small object half-buried in the drifting sand and dirt caught his eye, and he dismounted to look at it more closely. It was a rag doll, a somewhat grotesque rag doll, homemade, flour-bag material filled with sawdust, the face painted on crudely, wisps of cord for hair.

Cass Lorimer was standing there, holding the doll in his hands, his jaw hard, when he heard the riders coming up. They were swinging down a slope from the west, three of them, riding easily, coming straight toward the homestead. They'd either spotted his horse, or they'd seen him riding in a few minutes before.

Tossing aside the rag doll, Cass waited for them, one hand resting on the saddle, looking over the neck of the horse. Even before they came up, he was quite sure for whom they rode, even though this country was new to him. As one of the riders, a heavy-set, reddish-haired man swung his chestnut gelding around, Cass saw the Slash M on the hip. His gray eyes flicked a little, but his face was expressionless.

The red-haired man rubbed his flattened nose and said casually, "Figurin' on settlin' down here, mister?"

He had pale blue eyes, tough eyes, heavy jaws. He was a loose, hulking figure of a man, answering to the description Cass had of Ira Bream, ramrod for Slash M.

"Hard to say," Cass observed, "where I'll settle, my friend."

"Won't be here," the redhead grinned. "Slash M land, Buck."

Cass looked around leisurely, his eyes pausing for a moment on the rag doll he'd picked up. He said evenly, "Looks like a homestead to me."

He looked at the two men who had ridden in with the man with the red hair. They were nondescript riders, the kind you see lined up at a bar on a Saturday night in any cow town, dull-eyed men, tough because they were riding for a big outfit. One of them, a slack-jawed, yellow-haired youth of about twenty, said sourly, "Ask him his business, Ira, an' get him the hell out o' here."

Cass looked at the young man and smiled blandly. He said softly, "Let's see you get me the hell out of here." He glanced at the big redhead then, knowing that his guess had been right, and that this man was Ira Bream.

Bream said softly, "You're tough, Buck. Now maybe you can tell us what you're doin' on Slash M land."

"Just riding," Cass said. "Any law says I can't ride across open range?"

"You're not ridin' now," Ira Bream smiled. He hunched himself in the saddle, slipped a tobacco pouch from his shirt pocket, and started to roll a cigarette. His fingers were broad, thick, the backs of his hands covered with a reddish fuzz.

Cass looked around. He said, "Maybe I stopped for water."

"Maybe," the yellow-haired boy growled, "he's just snoopin', Ira."

"Maybe," Cass said to him, "you'd like to step down off that horse and have your face slapped." He looked steadily at the rider across the saddle, seeing the red come into his face. For one moment he thought the yellow-haired boy would accept his challenge, but instead of dismounting, he cursed. Cass just smiled at him, recognizing the oaths for what they were—futile sops to his pride.

Ira Bream said evenly, "In this country, Buck, we don't talk like that to Slash M riders."

"I'm not from this country," Cass reminded him.

"We ought to teach him a lesson," the yellow-haired boy snarled.

Cass just looked at him, and the derision was in his eyes again. He stepped into the saddle and he sat there, waiting for more questions before riding on. Ira Bream had one more query.

"What's your name?" Bream asked.

Cass looked at him thoughtfully. The name seemed to slip out of his mouth as if by impulse. It seemed to come naturally, possibly because that name was the last name with which he'd had any contact. He said, "Kincaid."

He was not prepared for the transformation which followed. Ira Bream's heavy jaw sagged. He stared at Cass, the half-rolled cigarette slipping from his fingers, tobacco spilling over the pommel of the saddle.

The yellow-haired rider turned gray. His lips worked spasmodically, and fear came into his eyes. Cass Lorimer had seen a rat look like that, cornered, seeking some way to run.

The third man, a short, dumpy rider with a flattened face and dull, slate-colored eyes, swallowed, rubbed his mouth with the back of his hand, and then for some reason took off his hat and began to dust it.

"Kincaid," Ira Bream repeated. "Ty Kincaid." He started to smile, then, recovering his composure, said hastily, "We—we figured you'd be along soon, Kincaid. Reckon we kind o' mixed you up with a loose rider. Griff Munson's been waitin' for you all week."

"Has he?" Cass murmured. He looked at the yellow-haired boy, and the rider licked his lips and acted as if he were trying to draw back into himself.

Ira Bream said hastily, "Arch, here, kind o' talked out o' turn, Kincaid. He's got a big mouth since he started ridin' for Slash M."

"He'd better get over it," Cass said.

"Just a kid," Bream assured him. "He didn't mean no harm, Kincaid."

Arch didn't say anything. He sat there, his face a mottled color, breathing a little easier now as if realizing that the climax was past. Deep down in his green eyes, Cass saw the hatred, but the fear rode herd on the hatred.

Another rider was coming up, and Cass, hearing the hoofbeats, turned his head slightly. A black horse with a white face came over a slight rise beyond the abandoned homestead, a hatless girl with copper-colored hair in the saddle.

Cass watched her curiously. She wore fawn-colored riding pants and a tan shirt to match. Her eyes were deep blue and very steady as she looked at Cass and the other men. She was pretty, but there was a kind of diamond hardness to her which Cass Lorimer did not quite understand.

Ira Bream said, "Afternoon, Miss McCoy."

He lifted his hand to his hat, and Cass did so, also, as he pulled the buckskin around. He noticed that Miss McCoy gave him a faintly curious glance.

Bream said, "Miss McCoy, meet Mr. Kincaid."

The girl on the black horse looked at Cass, nodded, and said to Bream, "Saw your horses.

I wondered what you were doing at the old Lorimer place."

Cass looked at the ruins of the homestead, and he said idly, "Maybe looking for ghosts, ma'am."

She gave him a little more attention. Then, looking at him squarely for the first time as if aware of the fact that he was no loose range rider like the other two with Bream, she said briefly, "It's a good place for ghosts." Turning to Bream, she said, "If you're picking up yearlings I spotted three of them up along the creek."

Bream nodded. "We'll run 'em in," he said.

It was then, for the first time, that Cass saw the gleam of derision and contempt in the eyes of the Slash M foreman. Glancing quickly at the other two riders, he caught that same, sly, derisive and yet interested expressions in their eyes as they looked at Miss McCoy. They looked at her the way men in a saloon looked at a notorious dance hall girl, and yet this girl did not appear to be that type at all, neither in dress nor manner. It was very strange.

As Miss McCoy nodded to them and turned her horse away, Ira Bream said to Cass, "Reckon Griff's waitin' for you, Kincaid. You ridin' in to the house now?"

Cass hesitated for one moment, and then shook his head, aware of the fact that now he had a part to play—possibly a very dangerous part, something he'd stumbled into quite by accident.

15

However, he'd taken the first step, and now there were others to take—steps which might lead him to that which he had traveled six hundred miles to find, or they might lead him to a dry gulch with a bullet in his back.

It was very evident that this man Kincaid had a character—a hard, tough, uncompromising character—and the very sight of him put fear into the hearts of men who'd never seen him, but who'd been intimidated by his reputation. The reason for the smooth, uncalloused hands of Kincaid, the dead man in the grove, was now quite clear to Cass. Ty Kincaid had been a gunhand—a professional gunhand, living by reason of the death he dealt out for pay. Kincaid, the drunk, the suicide, would not have been bossed around by even a man of Griff Munson's stature, and Munson was the owner of Slash M, the biggest cow outfit in this part of the country.

Cass said, "Well, I'll be in town if Munson wants to see me."

He knew after he'd said it that the remark had been in character. He saw the grudging admiration slip into Ira Bream's pale blue eyes. Apparently, in this country, men didn't tell Griff Munson he had to come to them. Ty Kincaid could do that and get away with it.

Bream nodded. "Reckon that'll be better," he admitted. "I'll tell Griff you're here, Kincaid. You can hole up at the Yankee House."

"I'll hole up," Cass said evenly, "where I damn please, mister." His eyes followed the black horse as it moved across open range. He noticed that Miss McCoy rode a horse the way a western girl would ride one, very loose in the saddle.

Ira Bream laughed uncomfortably. "No offense, Kincaid," he chuckled. "Yankee House is the only hotel in town."

Cass nodded. He gave the three men in front of him fleeting, contemptuous glances, and then he turned the buckskin and headed in the general direction of Red Rock, a lone figure, much like the drunken man who'd turned his horse off the stage road, had his last drink alone in a pine grove and then said good-by.

He rode tall and straight in the saddle, knowing that the three men were staring after him. He wasn't thinking about them—he was thinking about Miss McCoy with the copper-colored hair and the blue eyes like an October sky. Then his thoughts turned to the contempt and derision in the eyes of the Slash M riders. That was strange—very strange.

Chapter Two

He came into Red Rock at five o'clock in the afternoon as the sun reddened the windows of the buildings facing west. It was a small, scraggly, unpainted town, one, twisting main street, and a series of weather-beaten false-front buildings, with here and there a vacant lot, like a row of teeth with empty spaces.

The dust in the road was six inches deep, and there had been no rain here for a long time. The steady, unrelenting heat of late summer had beaten Red Rock into a kind of stupor. The horses at the tie racks in front of the stores and saloons drooped, swishing their tails idly at flies.

The few people on the boardwalks moved slowly, listlessly. It was as if the energy in them had been drained out by the heat of the sun, and they were waiting now for the revivifying rain.

Cass glanced idly at the store fronts as he passed by on the right side of the street. At the first intersection, occupying a conspicuous corner, was the office of the town lawyer. Cass read on the window the name in gold lettering, HILARY MANVILLE—ATTORNEY AT LAW.

He saw Manville behind the window, sitting at his desk, sprawled back in a swivel chair, facing the window, looking straight out at him through the letters.

From what Cass could see Manville was small, lean, gray and bespectacled. He was smoking, and the fingers holding the cigar were long, lean and bony, like claws.

Cass counted six saloons on the first block, and that was about normal for a town of this size. There was a dance hall, closed and padlocked at this hour, a few shops, a large dry goods and general store, and then the Yankee House, occupying the corner of Main and Grant streets, the only two-story structure in town, a rambling affair running north and west with a porch and a full balcony overhead.

Drab, yellowish curtains and sun-faded shades hung at the windows. A few drummers sat in the wicker chairs on the porch, fanning themselves, talking with the glibness of salesmen all over the world.

Dismounting in front of the Yankee House, Cass tied the buckskin to the rail, ducked under, and went up the steps. The drummers stopped talking to give him a searching glance, and then forgot him when he went inside.

The clerk at the desk was old, shriveled and scrawny. He wore a striped shirt with arm bands. Looking up at Cass, he said, "Afternoon."

Cass said, "You have a livery here?" When the clerk nodded, he went on, "The buckskin outside is mine. Have your hostler rub him down. I want good oats."

The old clerk grinned. "For yourself or the horse, mister?"

Cass just looked at him, remembering who he was supposed to be. The smile faded from the face of the old man, and he said rather gruffly, "You want a room here?"

"Cool side of the house," Cass told him.

"Ain't no cool side of any house in this town," the clerk said curtly. He turned the register book around and handed Cass a pen, and then he reached for a key from the board behind him.

Cass wrote the name down clearly, distinctly—T. Kincaid. He neglected to put down where he was from, leaving that space empty. Then he took a leather folder from his pocket and waited to pay in advance, watching the old man's face closely as he read the name.

It made no impression here as it had out at the homestead, and Cass thought curiously, *Only Slash M knows anything about it—whatever it is.*

"T. Kincaid," the clerk repeated. "Room Eleven—second floor. About eight o'clock tonight we begin to get a little cool air from the Estrellas to the north. You can open your window then. Open it sooner than that and you'll think you're sleeping in a furnace room all night."

"How much?" Cass asked.

"How long?" the clerk wanted to know.

Cass thought about that. "One week," he said.

"You can pay a day ahead," the clerk told him, "or you can pay for the whole week. Suit yourself, Mr. Kincaid."

Cass paid for the whole week, but even as he did so he was thinking rather ruefully that he might not be alive the whole week. It depended upon many things. It depended for instance on whether Griff Munson knew T. Kincaid, personally, or if he'd hired him—sight unseen. It depended upon the fifty-fifty prospect that no one else in Red Rock knew T. Kincaid.

He said to the clerk, "Where can I get a shave and a bath?"

"Barber shop next door," the clerk jerked his head to the right. "Cold water will be warm, though."

Cass put his money folder away. He said without smiling, "Will it?" He heard the clerk muttering to himself as he moved toward the door, and he smiled faintly.

The barber, a thin, bald man was communicative as Cass had expected. He'd had few customers this day, and he'd been sitting in the shade of the overhead awning when Cass stepped off the porch of the Yankee House and came down toward his shop. The barber said, "Stranger in town?"

"I could be," Cass told him.

"That buckskin," the barber observed, undaunted, "looks like he has plenty of bottom."

He began to work the lather into Cass's three-day-old beard.

"He has," Cass said.

"Come in from the north?" the barber wanted to know.

"South," Cass said.

"You'd o' seen them farmer's wagons on the flats," the barber told him, "if you'd come down from the north."

"Would I?" Cass murmured.

"Another whole flock of 'em," the barber went on glibly, assuming he'd hit upon an interesting point. "Headin' fer the land office this noon like a flock o' ducks. Must be about twenty of 'em."

"Nesters," Cass said noncommittally.

"How long will they last in this country?" the barber asked, posing with both lathered hands raised. "Ain't enough rain in this country to grow weeds." He wiped his hands on a towel and began to strop the razor. "Only water," he said, "wet enough to drink is on Slash M range."

Cass thought of the little stream which flowed past the homestead at which he'd met Ira Bream that afternoon. That was the only water he'd seen on this range, and evidently most of it belonged to Slash M.

"They'll last six months," the barber went on glibly, "or maybe some of 'em who are lucky might stick it out until they own their hundred and sixty acres, or they'll scrape up enough money to buy it from the government."

"Then what?" Cass asked. He lay back in the chair, looking up at the ceiling, the hardness coming into his eyes. He thought he knew the answer to that one.

"Then," the barber said a little more cautiously, "Slash M owns it. All of a sudden."

There was a lull in the conversation because this evidently was a risky topic, and the barber was not sure of Cass's politics.

Cass said, "Ran across a girl up on Slash M range. Miss McCoy."

He waited, leaving that bait dangling, and the barber was quick to snatch it up.

"Katie McCoy," he grinned. "Nice looker, wasn't she?"

"Reckon so," Cass agreed.

"Over on Slash M range," the barber purred, and that sly look was on his face, the same expression Cass had seen in the eyes of the Slash M riders. He felt tempted to push this man back and slap him across the mouth with the back of his hand. It was that kind of look.

"Her father was a nester," the barber began, and this topic pleased him immensely. On this he could range at will. He was a big, fat cat beginning to work on a hapless mouse. "Had a nice little place adjoining Slash M—water on it, too."

"They still there?" Cass asked him.

"Old Man McCoy pulled out," the barber said. "Wasn't much good to begin with, I guess. His wife died right around the time he sold out to Griff Munson."

Cass stared at him curiously. "The father left," he repeated, "and the daughter stayed on?"

"Has a new place," the barber leered, "right on the edge of Slash M range—the old Denson place, been fixed up. Lives there with an Indian woman housekeeper." He added, "Maybe you seen it comin' in?"

"No," Cass said. It was beginning to sift into his mind now, and it made him sick.

"Kind o' funny, ain't it?" the barber laughed slyly, "her takin' up so close to Slash M—livin' there—kind of alone."

Cass Lorimer understood those derisive, scornful looks. He voiced the next question slowly, deliberately, hating himself for doing it. He said, "Who paid to fix up the Denson place?"

The barber laughed again. "Now," he asked softly, "who do you figure would be payin' for anything like that, mister?"

Cass didn't say anything. He wondered why it should bother him, but it did. Griff Munson of Slash M had cattle; he had land; he had a big crew; and he had a woman. It was just that Katie McCoy didn't seem to be the kind of a girl you could buy like that.

"Griff Munson's a big man around here," the barber observed.

"That's right," Cass said. He thought for a moment, and then he said, "How long she been over at the Denson place?"

"Just a few weeks," the barber told him. "She was livin' at the hotel for a while after her father moved out of the country." He added, "Some talk around that old McCoy wasn't her real father. More like a stepfather, I'd say."

Cass didn't say any more on the subject. The barber would have liked to expand on this savory subject, but he received no encouragement from Cass.

"Plenty of other places she could have fixed up if she'd wanted to, not so near to Slash M," the barber said, leering.

"Fix up some bath water for me," Cass said evenly. When the barber opened his mouth to start in again, Cass said, "Now."

The barber left to set a few big kettles of water on the stove in the adjoining shed. When he was out of the room, Cass stared at his half-shaven face in the mirror on the wall. He scowled, and then told himself he was a fool to be concerned in this matter. He had his own business to attend to in Red Rock.

An hour later, seated in the bathtub, a cigar in his mouth, he wondered idly when Griff Munson would come into town. It was after six now—time for a man to be having his supper. He wondered if Griff Munson had some meals at the Denson place.

Taking the half-smoked cigar from his mouth, he stared at it distastefully for a moment, and then threw it against the tin wall of the shed. He heard a man moving past the shed on the outside, whistling tunelessly; he heard his boots making the boardwalk creak.

He got up then, dried himself and dressed, putting on a clean shirt he'd brought along for the occasion. He felt better when he paid the barber and went out onto the street.

It was nearly dusk now, and considerably cooler than it had been an hour or so earlier. That breeze the hotel clerk had spoken about had evidently started up earlier than usual.

Standing on the edge of the wooden boardwalk, his hands in his back pockets, Cass looked over the town for a moment before stepping into the hotel dining room. There were more horses at the tie racks now, and some of the saloons which had been empty when he rode in now had customers.

A man came down the walk behind him, and he heard that same tuneless whistle he'd heard in the tub. Turning his head slightly, he glanced at the whistler, and the first thing he noticed was the star—shining brightly in the gathering gloom.

The wearer of the star was tall, lank, rather thin shouldered. Cass had a good look at his face as he came up, a smiling, genial, bony face, a rather sharp nose which did not seem to go with the wide, humorous mouth.

The sheriff of Red Rock looked curiously at Cass as he came up, recognizing him as a stranger. He said, "Nice evening."

Cass nodded. The man wore a Colt gun, wore it rather low too, which could or could not mean anything. Men like Kincaid wore their guns low on the hip. He watched the sheriff pass on and enter the Plains Saloon. Then Cass went into the dining room which was off the lobby of the hotel.

He had a fairly good meal, steak, French fried potatoes and canned corn, along with two cups of hot coffee. He felt better when he got up from the table, paid his bill, and went into the lobby. On his way up to his room he passed a girl coming down the stairs.

The stairway was quite narrow, and Cass stopped, standing to one side to let her pass. He hadn't quite expected a girl like this to be staying at the Yankee House. The hotel seemed quite empty, and he'd supposed that only occasional cattle buyers or drummers stopped over. A town like Red Rock would not have too many out-of-town people.

She was an eastern girl, somewhat tall, slender, light, honey-colored hair and violet eyes—a beautiful girl. As he touched his hat to her, she nodded pleasantly. The way she held her head, and her carriage, indicated that she could be of English ancestry. Her complexion was English too, light, creamy, unlike Katie McCoy's brown, healthy skin. As she went by on her way down to the lobby, Cass caught the faint aroma of violets.

He went on up to his room, wondering what this girl was doing in a hotel like the Yankee House. It was rather remarkable that in a town as small as Red Rock and its environs he'd met two very unusual women in less than half a day.

In his room he took the Navy Colt .45 from the holster, emptied it, put in fresh cartridges, spun the cylinder a few times and slipped it back into the holster. He sat on the edge of the bed for a few moments, staring at the floor, and then before turning down the lamp and blowing it out, he stepped to the window.

A group of riders were moving past the front of the hotel, across a patch of light from the nearest saloon. He read the brands as they went by. They were all Slash M.

Chapter Three

Out on the street again it was considerably cooler. Some of the heat was still there, but it was being pushed back by the cooling breeze coming in from the mountains to the north. The dust was still as bad as ever. It was like ash dust, dry, gritty and powdery. When a rider moved past, his horse kicking up the alkali, it hung in the air, glittering like miniature diamonds, reflecting the light from the many saloons along the street.

Cass Lorimer waited until two horsemen moved past him, and then he crossed the street to the Plains Saloon. The tie rail here was crowded now, and he noticed that most of the brands were Slash M. There were others—Hatchet, Double A, Rail G, but Slash M was the big outfit.

Ira Bream was at the bar inside the Plains Saloon when Cass went in. Bream had his back to the wood, his elbows hooked over the edge of the bar, and he was chatting with two other men. He'd been watching the door, and Cass knew that he'd been watching for him, waiting for him.

There was a flicker of recognition in Bream's pale eyes, but that was all. Arch, the yellow-haired Slash M rider, was close at hand, sullen as usual, his thin face flushed with drink already even though it was not yet eight o'clock.

Cass looked at Bream, and then looked away again. He found an empty spot at the crowded bar, and he pulled in waiting until a bartender came up to him.

There were other strangers in the Plains Saloon tonight besides himself. Cass saw them along the walls, having an occasional drink at the bar, watching, listening, gaunt men with big, calloused hands and dusty, sweat-stained clothing—the farmers who'd come out to this part of the country to take up government land. These were the men upon whom Griff Munson fattened, letting them take up their land, prove it, and then squeezing them out when he was ready, especially those with good water rights.

Cass had his drink alone, and then he noticed that Bream was coming up, passing along the bar, nodding to acquaintances. The Slash M foreman said softly as he went by, "Griff's in the back room, waitin'."

He looked toward a door at the far end of the bar, and then he kept going, whistling, disappearing through the doorway, himself. Cass lighted a cigar. He puffed on it for a few moments, taking his time, and then he pushed away from the bar and headed for the door, wondering ruefully as he put his hand on the doorknob if he would sleep in the bed he'd paid for tonight, or if he'd rest on a slab in the coroner's shack.

The back room was a private gambling room

with several tables, only one of which was occupied. A big, smiling, red-faced man sat behind the table, playing solitaire, the cards spread out before him. Ira Bream sat back against the wall a little distance away, his chair tilted, the back of it braced against the wall. A third man was in the room, a Slash M rider, grizzled, stoop shouldered, a heavy gun on his hip. He took a position against the door, his back to it, after Cass came in.

The big man at the table said, "Kincaid?" He held out a hand. It was big, smooth, strong. He was a fine-looking specimen, over six feet tall, solid in the shoulders, solid in the body, but not fleshy. Smooth-shaven, his face was wide, strong-jawed, pale, turquoise eyes, good teeth.

His expensive Stetson was pushed back on his head, and his hair was ash blond, smooth. That was the impression Cass got of him—smooth and bland, that very smoothness containing an inner toughness.

Cass shook his hand, sinking down into the chair on the opposite side of the table. He turned his head slightly as he sat down to look at the puncher by the door, and he smiled.

Griff Munson said, with a grin, "Not to keep you in, Kincaid. To keep others out."

Cass relaxed a little. "Didn't figure you were trying to keep me in," he observed.

"Have a nice trip north?" Munson asked him. He took a cigar from his vest pocket, bit off the end, and put it in his mouth. Then he picked up the cards on the table and started to shuffle them aimlessly.

Cass said, "Fair."

"Heard you had a little trouble with some of our boys," Munson smiled. "They'll know how to handle you from now on, Kincaid."

"They'd better," Cass told him. He looked at Ira Bream, and Bream grinned uncomfortably.

"That damn Arch Cummings," Bream said. "He's got a big mouth since he works for a big brand."

"In El Paso," Cass murmured, "or Ellsworth, he'd last maybe a week."

Ira Bream guffawed, and Griff Munson puffed on his cigar for a moment. He said, "You think you'd do better staying in town rather than bunking out at Slash M?"

Cass looked at his fingers. "Who's the law in this town?" he countered. He was still in the dark here, feeling his way, and he had to walk carefully, never committing himself.

"Matt Quinn is sheriff of Red Rock," Munson said. "Kind of new. We haven't had any trouble with him as yet."

"He ain't had any with us, either," Ira Bream put in caustically.

Cass held his fingertips together. "I'll stay in town," he decided. Then he waited for Munson to go on, and Griff Munson said,

"There's still about a half dozen of them up along Wood Creek, this side of the old Lorimer place, where you met Bream. They're getting rather tough, even banding together. I tried to buy them out, but they turned me down."

When he mentioned the words, "Wood Creek," Cass noticed a very subtle change come over the man. His eyes seemed to be a trifle brighter, and a pulse started to beat in his temple. It was a very strange thing, and Cass filed this data away in the back of his mind for what it was worth.

He noticed that Ira Bream was leaning forward a little by the wall, moistening his lips, his pale blue eyes gleaming. Whatever it was, Bream was in on it.

Cass shifted his chair slightly so that he could glance at the third man in the room, the phlegmatic gunhand who stood by the door. He didn't know anything. He was here because he knew how to throw lead, and he was willing to throw it for pay. Wood Creek was just Wood Creek to him.

Cass said thoughtfully, "Nobody in your outfit could persuade them to sell?"

Griff Munson shrugged. "Been a little talk in town," he admitted. "More than I like. We've had trouble with nesters before, and I don't want the government coming out here."

Cass nodded. This legitimately explained why Munson was bringing in a hard case like Kincaid to front for him, but it did not explain Munson's tremendous interest in Wood Creek, and the homesteads along it. Munson had plenty of land, and he had plenty of water for his stock. Adding a few more hundred and sixty acre tracts to his domain might make him slightly wealthier, but it did not put much of a gleam in the eyes of an already prosperous rancher.

"Hilary Manville will handle the business end of it," Munson was saying. "He'll represent you in the deals. These six homesteads have all been proved or bought; you'll buy them from the nesters, set yourself up as a rancher, temporarily, and then turn the whole tract over to me in a legitimate business deal. In that way no one can point the finger at me, and you're out of the country."

"Suppose they won't sell," Cass pointed out. The deal was a pretty clever one as Munson had arranged it.

Munson laughed and shook ash from his cigar. "That's what I'm paying you for, Kincaid," he observed.

"How much?" Cass asked.

"Two thousand in cash when you turn those homesteads over to me," Munson stated.

Cass leaned back in the chair. "Must be pretty good grazing land up along Wood Creek," he said idly, and again he saw the change come over Griff Munson. The big man was still smiling, outwardly very relaxed, but his eyes were more narrowed, and that pulse was beating again. *For what?* Cass Lorimer thought. *For six homesteads!*

"I usually know what I'm buying," Munson smiled, "and the sooner the better. You could ride out to Wood Creek tomorrow."

"When I'm ready," Cass said, "I'll ride."

Griff Munson stared at him for a moment, his turquoise eyes seeming even a shade lighter. He looked as if he were going to take exception to this remark, and then he shrugged and smiled coolly.

"Your job, Kincaid," he said.

Cass went out into the saloon again. The Plains Saloon was quite crowded now. The half dozen card tables along the wall were filled, and there was no room at the bar. He noticed that Arch Cummings, the Slash M hand, was at one of the tables, playing grimly, sullenly, losing, and in a bad mood.

One of the players at Cummings' table attracted his attention. He had the feeling that he should have known the man, that he'd met him somewhere before, and then he realized that this was ridiculous because the man was evidently an easterner, and he knew no eastern men.

The card player was fairly tall, slender, light-haired, almost reddish in color, a light complexion. He was probably in his late twenties or early thirties. He wore a tweed suit and a bow tie, both of which were out of place in this town, and Cass wondered about him.

The easterner seemed to be having a good run of luck in the game too. As Cass watched from the wall he raked in another pot, adding to the fairly large stack of chips in front of him.

There were four players in the game, and one of them got up after this last pot, his chips gone. Cass hesitated for one moment, and then on an impulse picked his way between the other tables, coming up behind the empty chair. The easterner glanced up at him, smiling. He had light blue eyes, and a nice grin. When he spoke it was with a faintly clipped, precise manner, and Cass immediately identified him as English. There were occasional Englishmen in this western cattle country, many of them going into the stock-raising business or prospecting for iron or coal deposits.

"Sit down," the Englishman invited. He looked around the table, and smiled, "I presume you gentlemen do not mind?"

Arch Cummings stared at Cass grimly, but said nothing. He looked at the few chips in front of him, that surly expression on his face, like that of a small, spoiled child.

Cass dropped down into the chair. He signaled for the nearest waiter, gave him a bill, and waited for his chips. The Englishman was shuffling. He said to Cass, "Stranger in town?"

He evidently was not, himself. Cass just nodded. When his chips came, he put them in small piles in front of him, and then picked up the cards the dealer slid toward him.

"Schuyler is the name," the Englishman smiled. "John Schuyler."

"Kincaid," Cass said briefly. Beyond Schuyler he could see the bat-wing doors. They were opening now, and Matt Quinn, the sheriff of Red Rock, was coming in, lips pursed in that same tuneless whistle. Cass had a better look at the man in the light. Quinn had odd-colored, flinty eyes, sandy hair. He pushed his way through the crowd easily, his face expressionless, a tall, thin man with a bright star on his black vest. He wore a gray flannel shirt, and his hat was black, dusty. The heels of his boots were worn down, too, because a sheriff did a lot of walking around town.

Quinn spotted him at the table, let his eyes linger there for a moment, swing to John Schuyler and Arch Cummings, and then move away again.

Picking up his cards, Cass saw Quinn haul up at the bar, speak for a moment with a man there, and then move on. He came up behind John Schuyler a short while later on his way out of the saloon, slapped him gently on the shoulder as he went by, and said, "Run of luck tonight, John."

"About time," Schuyler grinned.

Sheriff Quinn went out, again glancing at Cass

curiously as he passed the table. Arch Cummings threw in the first hand. He said sourly, "You deal the damndest hands, Schuyler."

Even as he said this, Cass could see the quick gleam come into his greenish eyes. The words had evidently given him an idea, one he'd not had before. A cold grin slid across Arch Cummings' face, and then it was gone. He leaned forward a little at the table, resting his elbows on the wood, hands clasped, and then he said casually, "Takes a pretty clever man to deal out cards like that."

Schuyler glanced at him quickly to see if he were serious. His thin face flushed slightly, and then he smiled, accepting it as a joke. It was not a joke, though, as far as Cummings was concerned. He sat there, unsmiling, looking down at the table, and one of the other men at the table shifted uneasily.

"Let us hope," Schuyler said, "that your luck improves, my friend."

"Up to you," Arch Cummings stated, "when you deal, Schuyler."

Again the flush came to Schuyler's face. He dealt two cards to Cass when Cass raised two fingers to him, and then he put down the deck. He didn't say anything this time, but it was evident what Cummings was driving at.

Cass knew what he was coming to, also, and he'd seen it before. He'd seen Arch Cummings' type, too, before—many times—and he wondered how fast the Slash M rider was with a gun, and how accurate. Western killers of Kincaid's type usually started out as callow youths like Arch Cummings, surly, probably kicked around when they were children. Then discovering that they could handle a six-gun faster than most men, and shoot straighter, they made their first kill and then were off on bloody forays, mowing down one victim after the other, forcing their fights, living only for the moments when they could whip out their six-guns and blast someone down.

They became warped in their thinking, as Kincaid had. They hired out their gun to the highest bidder, and usually at a very early age they ran into someone who was slightly faster than they were on the draw, and their string of killings ended as their own names were added to the string of someone deadlier than themselves.

If they were particularly good, as Kincaid had been, they lasted longer, turning inward upon themselves, becoming reckless, eventually, turning to drink so that they would not have to think, to drop for a moment the eternal, tormenting vigilance which was the price they had to pay for the meager glory that was theirs.

Arch Cummings had not killed as yet. Cass was quite sure of that. There was speculation in his eyes as he looked across at John Schuyler, and not the killer's lust Cass had seen in the eyes of the typical gunfighter. Cummings wanted to know.

He may have practiced for a hundred hours with the heavy six-gun on his hip, drawing it in some desolate dry gulch, firing at tin cans, drawing and firing eternally, but never at a human target. Now he wanted to know.

Cass looked at his cards casually. He had two pair—aces and jacks. He raised the bidding, and Schuyler stayed in with him. Cummings watched moodily. He glanced over at Cass once in a while as if wondering what action he would take in any kind of trouble. Cass was supposed to be working with, if not for, Slash M.

It was about a twenty-dollar pot and Schuyler won it with three kings. As he raked in the chips, Arch Cummings said caustically, "Can't beat him when he deals, Kincaid."

Cass just looked at him, but didn't say anything.

Schuyler said flatly, "I don't like those remarks."

"Hell with you, then," Cummings grinned coldly.

It was a challenge, cool and deliberate. He sat there in the chair, letting his remark stand, defying Schuyler to do something about it. Cass wondered vaguely if John Schuyler had a gun on his person. If he did, there was little likelihood that he could use it with any degree of efficiency.

It was Cass's turn to deal. He picked up the deck, shuffled the cards and passed them out. He looked at Arch Cummings, then, and he smiled disdainfully, as if knowing what the Slash M rider was up to, then laughed at him contemptuously.

When Cummings drew nothing again and tossed his hand in, Cass said coolly, "Like my dealing, Arch?"

Cummings reddened. He sat there, his lips tight, knowing that the others had gotten the joke too. His chips were gone now, and he got up, mumbling, "I'm out."

He went away from the table, moving toward the bar, but Cass knew that he wasn't through with John Schuyler. Arch Cummings had to know, and tonight was the night he would know.

Schuyler glanced at Cass across the table, and he smiled faintly as if appreciating the joke. He wasn't being grateful to Cass for getting him out of what might have been a predicament because he was unafraid. Cass saw that in his blue eyes, and he liked the man for it.

They played for another hour, Cass breaking about even, before his interest waned in the game. He was restless tonight, anxious to be about the business of which he'd come to this town, but that was going to take time—time and caution. He had to be patient, to wait until he found out what he had to know, and after that his action was plain.

Arch Cummings was still in the saloon, watching another card game, moving to the bar occasionally to talk with another Slash M rider, and possibly to grub a drink. He was waiting, though, and always his green eyes shifted to John Schuyler.

When the game broke up, Schuyler said to Cass, "I'd like to buy you a drink, Mr. Kincaid."

Cass nodded. He noticed that Griff Munson was at one of the card tables now, and that Hilary Manville, the lawyer, was in on the same game. Manville glanced at him as he moved toward the bar, following Schuyler through the smoke-laden room. Manville had gray eyes to go with his gray color. His hair was thin and gray, and he was Griff Munson's man, body and soul.

"Staying in Red Rock?" John Schuyler asked as the bartender put a bottle and two glasses before them.

"Hard to say," Cass said briefly.

"Not too much doing here," Schuyler observed, "unless you're in the cattle business."

Cass wondered what he was doing in this town. He was not a drummer, and he didn't seem to be a cattle man.

"I've been here about six months," Schuyler observed, "doing a series of paintings for an English art concern."

"Paintings," Cass murmured. "You're an artist?"

John Schuyler smiled. "Not too much of a one," he stated modestly. "I'm doing western background scenes—cowpunchers in action, western cattle, scenery, thinks like that." He added, "Red Rock seemed like a typical cow town. My sister Valerie and I both liked it."

Cass Lorimer knew, then, what had made him think he'd seen John Schuyler before. He'd seen Schuyler's sister on the stairs at the Yankee House.

"Believe I met your sister at the Yankee House," Cass murmured. "You staying there?"

"Only place one can stay in Red Rock," Schuyler grinned. "You there, too?"

"Signed in this afternoon," Cass told him.

Hilary Manville had left the card game and was coming toward the bar, pulling into an open space next to Cass. He was coming over to talk.

"I learned," Schuyler was saying pleasantly, "that it's a bad practice asking a man his business in the west."

"That's right," Cass said. He said no more, and Schuyler laughed.

Manville said at Cass's elbow, "Mr. Kincaid?"

Cass turned his head slightly and looked into Hilary Manville's gray, unblinking eyes. The attorney was smiling. He said, "I believe we have a little business together, Mr. Kincaid."

Cass nodded to him. He noticed John Schuyler edging away from the bar, and Arch Cummings watching him from the far wall where he'd been standing for the past half hour, just waiting.

"A matter of real estate," Hilary Manville smiled. He had large teeth, yellowish, but straight.

"Reckon I'm looking for real estate," Cass said. He wasn't watching Manville now. He watched young Cummings push away from the wall, come through between the tables, and intercept Schuyler, who was heading for the batwing doors. Arch made a remark, and Schuyler stopped abruptly. They faced each other across an empty card table. The Slash M puncher's lips were twisted into an evil grin.

Cass Lorimer moved away from Manville. He walked easily, moving in between the tables, coming up behind Schuyler. He heard Arch Cummings say tersely, "Didn't like the way you were dealin' in that game, Schuyler. Could be that you arranged some o' them hands."

John Schuyler's neck was flushed. He stood across the table from Cummings, very stiff, hands at his sides. Players at some of the nearby tables were watching warily.

"I do not cheat at cards," the artist said quietly.

"You were winnin' pretty handily," Cummings grinned. "I'm just sayin' that maybe there was a reason for it."

Cass started to move around John Schuyler, pushing a chair away to go around the table. He saw Arch Cummings watching him, the worry coming into his green eyes.

Cass said, "You lost your money. Go on home now. Don't cry like a baby."

The Slash M rider flushed. The hatred welled

up in his eyes again. He said hotly, "This ain't your business, Kincaid."

"Making it mine," Cass told him. "Get out."

Arch Cummings hesitated, and Cass knew what was going on inside his mind. Young Arch was standing in front of a famous gunfighter. They both had guns on their hips of equal fire power. The bullets from one were as deadly as the bullets from the other. And Arch Cummings had been practicing his draw for a long time—on tin cans. He was wondering now exactly how fast Kincaid was, wondering if he could match his draw, or even beat him, thinking of the glory a first killing like this would bring him.

Cass stepped up to him, put a hand against his chest, and pushed hard. Arch cursed as he stumbled back against the table behind him. His right hand was down near the butt of the Colt on his hip, but he didn't put his hand on the gun.

The card players nearby scrambled back out of range, and Cass Lorimer started to walk in again, steadily, the contemptuous smile still on his face. It broke Arch Cummings' spirit; it quenched his desire to be a killer. He retreated, lips moving, the fear in his eyes. He backed out of the swinging doors.

He would still be dangerous, Cass knew, particularly to himself, but not in a stand-up fight. Arch Cummings would shoot from ambush now. He would never again have the nerve to stand up to another man with a gun in his hand."

Cass said to John Schuyler, "You headin' up to the hotel?"

The artist nodded. As they were walking out onto the porch he said, "I didn't have a gun, Mr. Kincaid."

"You're better off without one," Cass smiled, "unless you know how to use it pretty well."

"A fact to remember in this country," Schuyler chuckled. He said as they walked down the street toward the Yankee House, "Would you care to have dinner with my sister and me tomorrow, Mr. Kincaid? I feel that I owe you something for getting me out of that nasty spot."

"My pleasure," Cass murmured. Thinking of Valerie Schuyler, he was quite sure that it was going to be a pleasure.

Chapter Four

He met Valerie Schuyler the next morning instead of evening. Coming down to the hotel lobby after shaving and washing, he spotted John Schuyler and his sister just entering the dining room. The artist waved a hand to them, and Cass went over.

"My sister, Valerie," John Schuyler smiled. "Mr. Kincaid, the gentleman I spoke to you about last night."

Cass took off his hat. He noticed that her eyes were a deeper shade of violet than her brother's. She was smiling pleasantly, and she spoke in a low, modulated voice.

"John has been telling me about last night, Mr. Kincaid."

"Won't you join us for breakfast?" the brother asked him.

"Glad to," Cass nodded.

Sheriff Matt Quinn was eating alone in the dining room when they came in. He looked at the three of them curiously, and then nodded to Valerie Schuyler. Very clearly Cass saw that watchful look in his eyes, the expression of a man who has found a woman, and is a little wary of all other men thereafter. This came as a surprise to Cass.

John Schuyler said to his sister, "You planning on going to the dance tonight with Matt?"

"He hasn't asked me," Valerie smiled.

"Matt's slow that way," John Schuyler grinned. "He's probably digging up courage now." To Cass he said, "Have you met Sheriff Quinn, Mr. Kincaid?"

"Seen him around," Cass murmured. He wondered if he ought to try to beat Matt Quinn to the question, but he decided against it. Today he had to start finding the answer to his own question, and there was little room for a woman in his present plans.

Sheriff Quinn was finishing his coffee when they came in. He got up after he'd put the cup down and he came toward their table, touching his hat to Valerie Schuyler. Again he gave Cass that cautious look.

John Schuyler said to him, "Meet Mr. Kincaid, Sheriff."

"Seen him," Quinn nodded, running a hand through his sandy hair after he'd taken off his hat. He smiled in friendly fashion at Cass, and he repeated thoughtfully, "Kincaid?"

"That's right," Cass told him. He watched the sheriff's flinty eyes carefully, but was unable to read them.

"Seems like I heard that name before," Quinn murmured.

Cass just nodded. He noticed that Valerie

was smiling up at the sheriff pleasantly, and he wondered how it was between these two. He wondered, too, if this was just a diversion for Miss Schuyler. She was marooned in this cow town with her brother, and there was very little to do and not too many eligible men. He decided against this. Valerie Schuyler was too much the lady.

"Just wonderin'," Matt Quinn said, turning his hat around and around in his hands. "There's a dance on tonight run by the Cattlemen's Association. Figured you might like to go, Miss Schuyler."

"I'd love to," Valerie Schuyler said promptly.

He's afraid of me, Cass thought with some amusement. Then he wondered why it should be amusing and what Miss Schuyler's answer would have been had he put the question first.

Matt Quinn's face brightened up. It was not a particularly good-looking face, but when he smiled the change was most agreeable.

"Be around at about eight," he said, and he went on after nodding to Cass.

Cass watched him go, and he said, "How long has Quinn been sheriff of this town, Schuyler?"

"He was sworn in right after we arrived about six months ago," John Schuyler said. "I believe he'd been deputy sheriff a short while before that. The former sheriff left quite suddenly, right after one of the nesters was killed up along Stone Creek."

Cass Lorimer's eyes flicked. "You know the name of that nester?" he asked.

The artist thought a moment. "Man by the name of Jeff Lorimer, I believe," he replied. "Had a wife and a six-year-old girl."

Cass looked at the menu on the table. "They never found out who did the killing, I suppose."

Schuyler shook his head. Cass was conscious of the fact that Valerie Schuyler was looking at him curiously.

"He'd had trouble with some of the riders with one of the outfits," Schuyler explained. "Somebody shot him down just outside his house one night after they'd called him out. I don't know all the details, but Sheriff McElroy left shortly after the incident. Did you know Jeff Lorimer?"

"Saw his place when I rode in," Cass told him. "They burned it, too."

"After Lorimer's widow and child left," John Schuyler explained. "I believe Munson of Slash M eventually took title to the land at a public sale."

"It's part of Slash M range now," Cass said briefly. "Bream told me that."

"It was a terrible thing," Valerie Schuyler murmured. "We heard about it when we arrived. Some of the local homesteaders were quite bitter."

"Always been trouble between the ranchers and the homesteaders," Cass said evenly.

He noticed that John and Valerie Schuyler were watching him closely now, undoubtedly wondering at his questions. This was the beginning of a long series of cautious questioning, slow and careful probing, learning a little here and a little there, gradually drawing the noose tighter and tighter around the neck of the man who'd shot down his brother Jeff as he stood in front of his own home.

There was little doubt in his mind that Griff Munson had been behind the killing, and Munson would pay for his part of it. Possibly, Munson, himself had done the shooting, perhaps Ira Bream, or one of his riders. There was the possibility that Munson had brought in a hired killer of the Kincaid type and, if so, that man had to be tracked down. Whoever it was had to pay, and Cass Lorimer had dedicated himself to the task of squaring the debt if it took a lifetime to do it.

"Will you be at the dance tonight?" Valerie Schuyler asked, changing the subject.

Cass looked at her. "Hadn't thought about it," he admitted.

"One of the big events in town," John Schuyler observed. "I understand the Cattlemen's Association has this affair once a year. Just about everybody goes."

Cass thought of that. "Might as well be part of the town," he smiled. "Reckon I'll be there."

"Find yourself a girl to bring," Schuyler grinned. "I'm looking around, myself."

Cass arose to the occasion. Looking straight at Valerie, he said coolly, "From what I can see, most of the nice girls in this town are taken."

Valerie smiled at him, some color coming to her face. "Thank you," she said, and she seemed rather pleased with the compliment.

At nine o'clock Cass got up from the table. He said, "Figured I'd ride around the country a bit today. Always plenty to see in a new territory."

"Great cattle country," John Schuyler told him, "if you're interested in stock."

"I might be," Cass murmured. He nodded to Valerie, and he said, "See you at the dance."

As he left the dining room and went around the back of the Yankee House livery, he was thinking that Sheriff Quinn was a very lucky man. He wasn't quite sure about Quinn as yet. In a country like this, ruled by one big outfit, there was always the possibility that the sheriff was owned by that outfit too, despite what Bream and Munson had said.

The buckskin was well rested and anxious to go again. Cass saddled up, the hotel hostler watching his every move.

Then he said to the hostler, "Which is the shortest way to Wood Creek?"

He gathered that it ran north and west, parallel

with the stage road up which he'd gone, but he wasn't sure about that.

"You hit it six-seven miles southwest," the hostler told him. "Take the stage road. When you cross the wooden bridge over the gully you turn into Slash M trace. Foller that past Miss McCoy's place. Wood Creek is another mile."

There was that look in the hostler's eyes when he mentioned Katie McCoy. He was a small man, shriveled, narrow chin, bony face.

"I'll find it," Cass said.

He started to lead the buckskin out of the stable, and the hostler called after him softly, "Don't stop in at Miss McCoy's, mister."

Cass stopped. He stood there, looking back at the hostler, and then he said evenly, "Get your mind up out of the gutter, friend."

The hostler blinked. "A joke," he said weakly.

"This town," Cass told him, "should start looking around for a new subject for its jokes."

He mounted and rode out of the alley. Moving past Hilary Manville's office he remembered that he was supposed to stop in and see Manville. He kept going, grinning coldly. Manville could wait. Ty Kincaid would have kept him waiting.

He passed the morning stage coming up from the south, and the driver looked at him curiously as he rode by. Out of town he let the buckskin run a bit to get the excess energy out of its system. Going across the wooden bridge the hostler had mentioned, he turned up the trace which led to Slash M and Wood Creek beyond. A pile of stones marked the entrance way.

Moving up the trace he saw bunches of cattle with Slash M brand on the flank, fat, sleek cattle, well-fed, well-watered even in this dry spell. The range was not too crowded either, which made Munson's force buying of the six homesteads less and less plausible. He was going to great pains to get something which he did not need, and a man of Munson's brains did not go out on a limb like that. It was a mystery.

Another buckboard was coming down the slope ahead, greaseless wheels screeching, an old gray horse in the traces. A gray-haired man in worn, soiled overalls sat on the seat, a dark-haired boy beside him.

As the buckboard came down the grade, Cass distinctly saw the driver take a rifle from behind him and slide it across his lap. Both man and boy stared at Cass tersely as they went by. They looked at the brand on the buckskin's hip.

Homesteaders from Wood Creek, Cass thought. This was one of the men he was supposed to drive out. He wondered how much Hilary Manville would offer them for their hundred and sixty acres on which many of them had probably sweated the full five years proving time, or who had borrowed and scraped together the dollar and a quarter per acre price the government put upon these public lands opened to the homesteaders.

Ty Kincaid had to be paid out of the profits made on these homesteads, and Manville, himself, undoubtedly would get a cut. With these expenses in mind Griff Munson wouldn't be offering too much to the nesters for title to their lands.

Cass nodded to the farmer as he went by. He was given a curt nod in return by the tight-lipped man even after the nester had ascertained that Cass didn't ride for Slash M.

The land lifted after leaving the stage road, rising in a series of grassy hills. Here and there clumps of timber dotted the ridges, and everywhere Cass saw cattle. He spotted two riders bringing in a bunch of them from the west. The Slash M men didn't see him, and they soon disappeared over a rise.

Another rider, however, approached Cass from the south and, watching him closely, Cass recognized Ira Bream's chestnut gelding. Bream came straight toward him, lifting a hand. He swung in beside Cass, and he said, "You're out early, Kincaid."

Cass nodded, not liking this company, but unable to think of a way in which he could get rid of the man. He wondered if Munson had placed Bream here to watch for him, possibly to ride out with him wherever he was going.

"Headin' up for Wood Creek?" Bream asked.

"Munson want to know that?" Cass snapped.

Bream licked his lips. "Hell," he grinned, "just a question, Kincaid."

"I don't like watch dogs," Cass told him thinly. "If Munson sent you out here to watch me, you better start riding the other way, Bream."

Ira Bream slowed down. He scratched his head under his hat, and he said, "We heard you liked to play a lone hand, Kincaid. You don't want company an' I'll ride the other way."

"I don't want company," Cass said.

The Slash M foreman shrugged, swung the chestnut around, and rode the other way. Cass kept going without looking behind him, riding slowly, making a cigarette as he did so.

It was nearly high noon when he saw the Katie McCoy place, off to the right half-hidden in a clump of cottonwood along the edge of a small stream. There was wash on the line behind the house—the kind of wash a woman would have out, dresses, petticoats.

Cass pulled up, the cigarette half-smoked now. He sat there, looking at the house. It was a fairly respectable little frame building, one story, probably three or four rooms in it, a bit of porch in the front and a kitchen shed in the rear.

There was a garden, too, on the other side of the stream, and a small wooden bridge across the stream. An Indian woman was in the rear hanging up wash. She was short, dumpy, black haired.

Cass was wondering if Katie McCoy were in, and wondering if he had any reason for stopping, when the girl, herself, appeared in the doorway. She was wearing the same fawn-colored riding pants, but this time with a white silk blouse.

The sight of that silk blouse made Cass's jaw harden. He thought tersely, *A nester girl with a silk blouse and expensive riding pants. Who paid for them?*

Katie McCoy looked at him coolly from a distance of about fifteen yards. The trace to Slash M went past her doorway, but she was supposed to be on her own land, not Slash M range.

He felt foolish, just looking at her and then riding on, and he turned the buckskin down the road which led to the door. She stood there against one of the porch posts, watching him as he tossed away the cigarette.

Cass said, "I'm new in this country. Wood Creek up this way?"

Katie McCoy nodded toward the stream beyond. She said, "This stream runs into it."

He noticed her eyes more closely this time. They were blue, hard, cold and inflexible. She said, "You're the new rider for Slash M." It was almost an accusation the way she said it.

Cass shook his head. "I don't ride for any one," he stated.

"Bream said you were working for Slash M," Katie McCoy observed.

"Bream was wrong," Cass told her.

The girl looked at him thoughtfully. She said, "Don't tell me you're taking out land along Wood Creek. You don't look like a farmer."

Cass smiled faintly. "I'm new in this country," he repeated. "Just looking around now, ma'am."

Katie McCoy studied him thoughtfully for a moment. Then she said, "Coffee's on, if you want any."

The invitation came rather as a surprise to Cass. He hesitated for one moment before replying, and he thought he saw a kind of sardonic humor slide into the girl's hard eyes. He took one boot from the stirrup then, and he nodded.

"Much obliged," he said.

She went into the house as Cass walked the buckskin over to a small corral and tied it to the pole. The smell of frying eggs was in the air, and even though he'd had a rather late breakfast and wasn't particularly hungry, the eggs smelled good.

The house was nicely furnished and clean. There were rugs on the floor, curtains at the windows, and some pictures on the walls. This was not the sod shanty of a nester girl. There was even two pieces of upholstered furniture.

He saw Miss McCoy out in the kitchen, and when she heard his step on the floor she called over her shoulder, "In here, Mr. Kincaid."

The Indian woman glanced at him, her greasy

face expressionless. She'd set two places at the table, and then she shuffled out into the yard again to hang up her wash.

Cass sat down at the table, wondering how many times Griff Munson had sat here, hating the man the more for it. He watched Katie McCoy pour the coffee, and he noticed that her hands were brown and firm. He said after he'd tasted the coffee, "You're a good cook."

There were eggs and bacon and biscuits on the table. She nodded and smiled a little at his compliment, and when she smiled some of the hardness left her face. He wished he could have known her before she'd changed, when she'd been still a nester girl.

"Been in this part of the country long?" he asked.

"Since I was ten," Katie told him.

"Like it?" Cass wanted to know.

"Hate it," she said.

Cass frowned a little. "Why don't you get out?" he asked. "No law says you have to stay."

She sipped the hot coffee, looking at him over the cup, and the hardness was back in her eyes. "I'll get out," she said, "when I'm ready."

The answer made no sense, and Cass shrugged. He said casually, "Funny place for a girl to be living."

He shouldn't have said that because he saw

anger blaze up in her eyes. She said thinly, "You've been hearing stories in town."

Cass looked at her steadily. "Everybody talks," he stated.

"About something like this, with relish," Katie snapped.

Cass didn't say anything to that. He went to work on the bacon and eggs, and then he said, "You've got a nice place here."

"I like it," Katie told him. "I like it better than living in town. I'm not a town girl." She was watching him as he ate, and then she said, "You look like someone I used to know, but I can't place him."

Cass smiled. "That right?" he murmured.

"I'll remember some day," she said, "and then I'll know why you came here. Bream says you're working for Slash M. You say you're not. You don't say what you're doing."

"That's right," Cass nodded. He found himself hating Griff Munson more and more as he sat opposite this girl, hating him for what he'd done to his brother Jeff, for what he'd done here. He said suddenly, "I'll tell you what I'm doing tonight, Miss McCoy."

"What's that?" she asked curiously.

"Figured I'd go to the Cattlemen's dance," Cass said blandly, "If I had someone to go with me." He'd come out with it, and he watched her face now, knowing that the invitation had come almost as a shock to her. No one in this country ever asked her out. No one dared asked her out.

She said slowly, "The Cattlemen's dance."

"I'm new here," Cass smiled evenly. "I don't know many women. Now I know you."

She looked at him. "Do you?" she asked.

"I'm asking you," Cass countered. He wasn't sure yet what her answer would be. He expected a refusal, but she said suddenly, "I'll go."

Cass sat there, looking at her for a few moments across the table. Then he picked up his hat. He said, "Be around with a buckboard at about seven, if that's all right with you."

"All right," Katie McCoy murmured.

"And don't worry," Cass told her.

She looked at him, her face grim, pride in her eyes. "I never worry," she retorted.

Cass smiled as he went out. She didn't follow him to the door. He said, "See you," and he went out into the sunshine. He saw Griff Munson sitting astride a big bay horse, smoking a cigar, his horse standing in the trace which led to Slash M.

Munson was looking at the house, looking at Cass's buckskin tied at the corral. When he saw Cass come out of the house, his eyes lifted a bit, but that bland smile was still on his face.

Cass untied the buckskin, stepped into the saddle, and walked the horse out to the trace. Griff Munson was watching him calmly, puffing on the cigar. When Cass came up, he said, "I was wondering whose buckskin that was."

"Now you know," Cass told him.

Munson took the cigar from his mouth and grinned. "You know Miss McCoy, too," he murmured. There was no smile in his turquoise eyes. He sat there, holding the cigar in one of his smooth, strong hands as the bay shifted a little.

Cass saw the Colt gun on his hip, and he wondered how tough Griff Munson was with that gun, or did Munson shoot in the dark, possibly shoot at an unarmed man who'd stepped out of his home, leaving his wife and child inside, never to return again.

"I met Miss McCoy yesterday," Cass said. "Bream introduced me."

"I see," Munson nodded. He put the cigar back in his mouth and he said, "You talk to Manville this morning?"

"No," Cass told him. He looked at Munson calmly as if asking the boss of Slash M to make an issue out of it if he wanted to.

Griff Munson's eyes narrowed slightly, but he was still smiling. His voice was even, unemotional. He said, "Reckon you know your business, Kincaid."

"Reckon I do," Cass said. He turned his horse around and started to move past Munson, and as he did so he said softly, "If you were figuring on a partner for the dance tonight, Munson, Miss McCoy's already taken."

He rode on then without even waiting to see the effect on Griff Munson's face. It was not a great matter. It was a small thing, like the planting of the tormenting *banderillas* in the neck of the charging bull in the Mexican bullfighting arenas. *It was a small thing, but the bullfighters eventually disposed of the bull!*

Chapter Five

From the clerk at the Yankee House, Cass discovered that the Ace High Livery rented buckboards, and he walked down to the stable after having his supper in the hotel dining room with John and Valerie Schuyler. The supper had ended on a rather strained note. John Schuyler had put the laughing question to him.

"Find a girl for the dance tonight, Mr. Kincaid?"

Cass had nodded, and he saw Valerie Schuyler glance at him curiously.

"You didn't waste much time," Schuyler had chuckled. "Who is she?"

"Miss McCoy, from up near Wood Creek," Cass said casually.

There had been a moment of stunned silence, indicating that they, too, knew about her. He'd been quite sure that they would know about it. In a thinly populated country like this the McCoy-Munson scandal would have penetrated into every corner.

Valerie Schuyler had flushed a little, and then gone on eating in silence. Her brother had tried to talk it off, talk around it, but it was a big boulder in the pathway. He said, "Didn't know you knew her, Mr. Kincaid."

"Met her yesterday," Cass told him blandly. He

lighted a cigar when he'd finished eating, and then he'd added, "Seemed like a nice girl."

"I—I'm sure she is," John Schuyler told him, too hastily.

Cass had to smile walking down the hot, dusty street now. Valerie Schuyler had been virtually silent the remainder of the meal, and she'd seemed quite glad when Cass got up with the remark that he had to see about the renting of the buckboard.

The sun was nearly gone now, but it was still too early for that cooling breeze from the Estrellas. The heat was oppressive. It seemed to weigh down, to drain the energy out of the body.

The sky was turning to black velvet after the orange and the red had been flushed away, but there were no clouds. More of this stifling heat was in store for them on the morrow, and the days to come. Already, Cass had heard the nesters were talking of getting out. Those with plenty of water were making half-hearted attempts to irrigate their crops, but the others had to just sit and wait it out, hoping that the heat spell would be broken before their crops died.

The Ace High Livery was on Lincoln Street, two blocks south of the Yankee House. Cass could hear the dried boards crack beneath his weight as he moved past store fronts and dwelling places on Main Street and turned into Lincoln.

Although it was quite early in the evening he

noticed that there were quite a few horses at the tie racks in front of the saloons, and buckboards were coming in from the surrounding countryside. This Cattlemen's annual dance was an affair attended by practically every one. He wondered sardonically what the reaction would be when he drove up with Katie McCoy at his side. He wondered, too, if Griff Munson would make his appearance.

The owner of the Ace High was a fat man by the name of Farrel. He had a buckboard and a pair of nice chestnuts to go with it.

"Got a lady for the dance, mister?" the fat man asked genially.

"Reckon I have," Cass nodded.

Farrel spat and he said softly, "Bet I can tell you who Griff Munson will be bringin'."

Cass stepped up on the buckboard and picked up the reins after Farrel had put the chestnuts into the harness. He was still smoking the cigar he'd lighted at the supper table with the Schuylers. He said, "Don't bet on it, friend."

"This I'll bet on," Farrel leered.

Cass drove off. He had to swing out on to Main Street again and go all the way through it and out the south end of town, passing by the Yankee House. John Schuyler was sitting in one of the wicker chairs as he went by, and he lifted a hand to the artist. Schuyler waved back.

Valerie was nowhere in sight, and he wondered

if she were watching from the window. He wondered, too, if he hadn't made a mistake in inviting Katie McCoy to the dance, flaunting her in the face of Valerie Schuyler. He wasn't interested in Katie, considering the fact that she belonged to Griff Munson, and he was but slightly interested in Valerie Schuyler. Then thinking of Katie again he became somewhat confused.

He passed Sheriff Matt Quinn on his way down to the hotel, and Quinn looked at him, at the buckboard, and nodded. Quinn, too, was probably wondering whom he had invited to the dance, the buckboard being proof that he did have a partner.

Yellow lights were flickering on in the houses along Main Street as Cass took the buckboard up the grade out of town. He'd noticed that the dance hall was already illuminated, and a number of buckboards were tied in the alley adjoining it. A few lone punchers had been lounging about near the entrance way. Somewhere in the rear of the big, shedlike structure, Cass had heard the musicians warming up.

It was cooler out of town, and now the breeze was coming up. He sat back on the seat, his body rolling gently with the bumps and the hollows in the road. He passed several buckboards coming toward him, one of them filled with a swarm of children in the rear. Groups of riders, and lone riders, came out of the night, passing him, and he took their dust in his nostrils as he headed south.

A short while after he turned off the stage road, following the smaller road which led up to Wood Creek, he raised the lights of Katie McCoy's place.

She came out of the house when she heard the buckboard coming up before the door, and Cass sat there, staring at her for a moment before getting off the seat. She was dressed in white with a blue sash around the waist. He could see her very clearly in the lamplight which flooded the little porch. She had her hair done up differently too, and it seemed to glisten in the light. A sapphire brooch sparkled at her throat.

Cass said, "Am I on time?"

"You're punctual," Katie told him. "You have time for another cup of coffee if you wish, before we leave."

"It would taste good," Cass nodded. He went inside, and he saw the Indian woman in the kitchen again. The coffeepot was on the stove, and he wondered if it was always there, always boiling—for someone.

Katie said, "I *could* have invited you for supper. I didn't think of it. You eat at the hotel?"

Cass nodded again. "With John and Valerie Schuyler," he said. "You know them?"

She'd started to pour the coffee for him, and she stopped now to look at him. She said evenly,

"The artist and his beautiful sister. You know the nice people in this town."

Cass smiled. "Some of them," he agreed.

"And some," Katie McCoy added quietly, "who are not so nice. Isn't that right?"

Cass looked at her. "Why keep kicking yourself around?" he asked.

"Why did you ask me to the dance tonight?" she wanted to know, and he could see that this question had been rolling around in her mind probably since he'd left her.

He shrugged and he said, "Why does any man ask any woman to go out with him?"

"That's no answer," she said.

Cass sipped his coffee. He looked around the room, and he said, "It'll have to do, Miss McCoy."

Katie McCoy watched him from the other side of the table. She said quietly, "I might have my reasons for going with you, too, mister."

A faint smile slid across Cass's face as he set the cup down. He said, "Suppose tonight we just forget the reasons and have a good time."

"I can do it," Katie agreed.

Cass got up. Outside, he helped her into the buckboard and they drove away. There was a faint, yet disturbing aroma of perfume about her, and he wondered if she used that for Griff Munson too. The thought made him silent.

Katie said, "If this hot spell doesn't break soon

it'll be a tough winter for the homesteaders."

"Reckon most of the winters and most of the summers are tough on them," Cass nodded. "You found that out."

Katie McCoy was quiet for a moment. "We'd have made out," she murmured. "We had a good piece of land."

They didn't say any more on the subject. When they came into the stage road down below, they swung in behind another buckboard, and the occupants kept looking behind them to see who was in Cass's wagon.

Cass said softly, "Be a little talk tonight, Miss McCoy."

"Let them talk," Katie murmured.

Cass let the chestnuts move at an easy pace, preferring that the dance hall be quite filled when they got there. The other buckboard pushed on ahead, disappearing over a rise, and Katie McCoy said, "Are we making the grand entrance?"

"You catch on quickly," Cass grinned. "Reckon they're all going to look at us. We'll let 'em look all at once."

They could hear the music when they started down the grade. The outside of the dance hall had been rigged up with a dozen lanterns, providing plenty of light. There was the usual crowd of punchers outside the entrance way, smoking, talking, and as usual a bottle or two was being passed around. Three riders swept down past

Cass's buckboard as he entered the town, whooping, kicking up dust, pulling up abruptly in front of the dance hall.

As Cass came up, turning the buckboard into the alley, heads turned to see who the new arrivals were. There were about a dozen men out here, and they'd been joking, laughing. The noise suddenly stopped. Heads swiveled as Cass turned the buckboard into the vacant lot off the alley, driving in between two other vehicles parked here.

He stepped down and gave his hand to Katie. She came down nimbly, putting one hand on his shoulder. He didn't expect her to take his arm as they walked toward the entrance way, but she did.

The punchers around the doorway made room for them. They were still staring, and Cass heard one of them say softly, "Griff here yet?"

They went inside. The dance hall was well filled and couples were out on the floor. It was a long, rectangular building with a loft overhead. At one time it had probably been a stable, but since converted to a dance hall. There was a low railing around the dance floor proper, some tables and benches on the other side of the railing.

Many of the family groups had brought food with them, and it was already set out on the tables. The usual swarm of small boys climbed and clambered around the railings, or chased each other around the place.

Along one wall was the stag line, a dozen or so hopefuls, waiting for dances with the single, unattached girls. Arch Cummings, sullen as usual, a cigarette dangling from his mouth, was in this line, leaning against the wall. He let the cigarette sag a little when he saw Cass come in with Katie McCoy.

There were plenty of others who saw them come in too, and Cass felt their eyes on them as he led Katie out on the floor. She danced well, as he'd expected. She was light on her feet.

As they moved down the floor they passed Valerie Schuyler and Sheriff Quinn. Quinn danced woodenly, stiffly. He nodded to Cass and he noticed Katie, but there was no particular expression on his face.

John Schuyler was also dancing with a girl Cass did not know. He seemed to be enjoying himself and he nodded gayly to Cass, smiling also at Katie.

When the music stopped and they left the floor, Katie said, "I have one friend in town. Do you mind if I go over and talk to her?"

She nodded toward a plain, brown-haired girl, standing near one of the tables.

"She's a dressmaker in town," Katie explained. "Amy Murchison."

"Go ahead," Cass told her. "I'll be around." He saw Griff Munson and Ira Bream coming through the door. Munson had the usual cigar in his mouth and he was smiling. He looked at Cass and Katie together, still smiling broadly, and then he and Bream joined several other cattlemen who were having a chat on the other side of the dance floor.

Already, people were looking at Cass and at Munson, wondering what was going to happen. Cass lighted a cigar and leaned against one of the dance hall pillars as Katie moved away to talk with Amy Murchison. He noticed that Munson took up a position in the group across the hall so that he could look across the room and keep an eye on Katie and himself.

John Schuyler came up then, always pleasant. He said, "Enjoying yourself, Mr. Kincaid?"

"A nice affair," Cass nodded. He was watching Katie as she chatted pleasantly with the dressmaker, and as she spoke now she seemed more like a young girl, and not the hard-eyed woman he'd met that first afternoon at the homestead, nor the reserved, calculating woman he'd taken to the dance tonight.

John Schuyler was saying rather hesitantly, "You're new in this part of the country, Mr. Kincaid. I wouldn't like to see you have any kind of trouble tonight, so I'd better tell you this."

"What?" Cass asked.

Schuyler frowned, and he looked as if he wished he'd kept quiet. "It's just this," he blurted out. "I understand Miss McCoy is Griff

Munson's lady friend, and Munson is a big man around here. He might resent the fact that you're out with his girl."

"He won't," Cass said calmly.

John Schuyler stared at him. He said, "You—you know about it?"

"I know about it," Cass nodded. He puffed on the cigar and he looked serenely around the room.

Schuyler swallowed. "I see," he murmured, yet he saw nothing. "Just thought I'd tell you, Mr. Kincaid."

"Much obliged," Cass nodded.

He noticed that Sheriff Quinn and Valerie Schuyler were moving toward them at the edge of the dance floor. Valerie was dressed in blue this evening, shimmering blue which accentuated the color of her eyes. She was a beautiful woman as she moved alongside the tall, angular Matt Quinn, and Cass saw the eyes turn in her direction. Even Katie McCoy, talking with the dressmaker, turned her head slightly, tacit admiration in her eyes. Valerie Schuyler was a lady. She was not pretending to be one.

When the English woman smiled and nodded to Cass he was conscious of a quickening of the pulse, and again he was aware of that small hostility in the eyes of Matt Quinn.

Valerie said, "Enjoying yourself, Mr. Kincaid?"

"It's a nice affair," Cass nodded. "It'll be nicer if you'll save me a dance later in the evening."

Valerie smiled. "I'd be glad to," she said, and Matt Quinn stirred restlessly, looking past Cass, looking out through the open door to where the single punchers were talking boisterously, passing that bottle a little more frequently now.

Cass said to him, "Expecting trouble, Sheriff?"

"Always trouble at these affairs," Quinn told him. "Too much liquor around and not enough women."

John Schuyler laughed. "That seems to be a common failing in the West," he chuckled.

They stood there, talking idly for a few minutes, and Cass saw Matt Quinn glance across the dance floor at the group of cattlemen, with Griff Munson looming above them, his ash-blond hair slicked back, smooth shaven, big, strong hands shoved in his back pockets, the cigar tilted toward the ceiling.

It was hot and stuffy in the dance hall and, just before the music started up again, the sheriff of Red Rock and Valerie Schuyler stepped outside for a breath of air.

Katie McCoy came back as the couples were moving out on the floor. She said to Cass, softly, "You know Miss Schuyler. Why didn't you ask her to this dance?"

Cass shrugged. "I asked you."

"And now," she pointed out, "you're not even

worried about Griff Munson. I don't understand that."

"Let Munson worry about me," Cass said evenly. Katie McCoy looked up into his face queerly, her brows knit. "Keep your mind on your dancing," Cass said.

Katie laughed brittlely. "I didn't come here just to dance," she told him.

"I know that," Cass smiled faintly. He was quite sure why she'd accepted his invitation. She had to show Griff Munson and this town of Red Rock that she still had a few last shreds of self-respect. For what it was worth, she wanted to flaunt this tattered flag in Munson's face.

Later in the evening Cass had his dance with Valerie, and John Schuyler, a little ill at ease, took Katie McCoy out on the floor.

Valerie danced beautifully, as Cass knew she would, and once again the eyes followed them. People were wondering who he was, and why he'd taken it into his head to buck Griff Munson.

Valerie said as they were dancing, "Miss McCoy is a remarkably fine-looking girl."

"She is," Cass agreed, and Valerie said no more on the subject. He wasn't sure if it was because she did not particularly like his quick assent to her remark, or because there was nothing anyone could say on this delicate topic.

Sheriff Quinn was close at hand when they finished the dance. Cass had to smile a little at the sheriff's caution. He thanked Valerie for the dance, when he saw Katie McCoy chatting with Amy Murchison again, he drifted toward the door, lighting a cigar as he went outside.

Ira Bream was standing just outside the entrance way, a cigarette in his mouth, hands in his pockets, leaning against the wall. He nodded to Cass, and he said, "Nice night, Kincaid."

Cass just nodded. He moved past Bream and he took a position along the wall near the corner of the building. He could see couples strolling around out in the shadows, and he could hear their low talk. The crowd of lone punchers who'd been in the front were now down in the darkened alley where the buckboards were parked. He could hear their loud talk as the bottles went around.

He wondered where Griff Munson had gone. Griff had had a dance with a girl in the hall, and then he'd disappeared. Very possibly he'd gone down the street to sit in at one of the card games. He hadn't gone near Katie McCoy all evening.

Ira Bream, standing a few yards away, tossed his cigarette into the dust and then headed up the street. Cass saw Sheriff Quinn come outside with Valerie Schuyler, and then the bunch of loose punchers straggled out of the alley. They were laughing boisterously, and Cass Lorimer heard one of them say, "Figure I'll be runnin' up to that place myself some day. Maybe I ain't as good lookin' as Griff Munson, but looks ain't everything."

Another man was singing, "Katie—Katie—"

He stopped suddenly as they swung around the corner into the light and saw Cass looking at them from a few yards away. The man who had been singing was a pretty big fellow, light haired, heavy jawed, his hat on the back of his head. He was looking straight at Cass as he came around the corner, and in that instant Cass knew the man had been aware of the fact that he'd been there, and that the remarks and the singing were for his benefit.

He remembered that Ira Bream had been standing here a few moments before, and that Bream had flipped away his cigarette when Cass came out. That could have been the signal for these tough cowhands to go into their act. Griff Munson must have been a little peeved, or possibly he just wanted to find out how tough his hired gunhand was.

Chapter Six

There were ten in this group which had come out of the alley, and all of them were looking straight at Cass, making it very evident that they'd known he'd been standing there. It was all a little too pat the way they'd swung around the corner of the building and then stopped as one man.

Cass didn't move from his position at the wall. He spoke around his cigar, and he said, "You have a pretty voice, my friend."

The light-haired puncher eyed Cass deliberately. He'd had a few drinks, but he wasn't drunk, and if Griff Munson had hired this man for the little job he'd had in mind he'd picked a good one. The rider was big, solidly built, evidently a rough man with his hands. He probably was not a Slash M hand, either, because the Slash M men knew about Ty Kincaid and wouldn't dare pick a fight with him.

The puncher said evenly, "What's wrong with you, Jack?"

"When you sing again," Cass told him, "don't use that name again."

"What name?" the puncher grinned, and he came a step closer, his hands hooked in his gunbelt.

"You know damn well," Cass snapped, and

he was getting angry now—not so much at this young puncher, who was just a hired tough and liked to display his prowess with his fists, but at Griff Munson who kept a woman and then permitted her name to be dragged in the dust.

Ira Bream was coming back, a look of mild interest on his face. He was acting dumb, but he hadn't gone very far after tossing away his cigarette. He took up a position a little to one side of the group, his hat pushed back on his head.

The tall puncher said, "I use any name I want, mister, an' to hell with you." He grinned broadly, opened his mouth, and sang, "Katie—"

Cass Lorimer slapped him across the mouth with his left hand, at the same time ramming his right shoulder against the puncher's chest and snatching at the gun in his holster. He managed to whip the gun out and he stepped back, leveling it.

His own gun he'd checked at the door, but the men outside had not come in and they'd retained their guns. He stood there, the gun in his hand, and he said quietly, "Turn around and walk to the back."

The tall puncher stared at him for a moment, at the gun in Cass's hand. He'd been a little taken back by the swiftness of Cass's attack, but he was recovering his composure now. He said tersely, "You're pretty rough with your hands, Jack."

"I can be rougher," Cass told him. "Turn around and walk."

He didn't see Sheriff Quinn any more, and he wondered if, when Quinn heard about this fight, would he make any attempt to stop it. The puncher laughed and turned around. He walked down past the wall of the dance hall, Cass following him, and the crowd coming after them.

A man yelled in through the open door of the dance hall, "Fight!"

Boots clattered on the wood, and Cass could hear them tumbling outside as he followed the tall man to the rear. He didn't particularly care for this, but there was little that he could do about it now. He'd committed himself by taking Kincaid's name, and now by making a play for Griff Munson's girl. He had dealt his own hand and he would have to play it.

There was a cleared space behind the dance hall, and the moon was bright now, giving them plenty of light. When the puncher turned around and faced Cass, Cass tossed the gun aside. He took off his vest.

The crowd circled around them excitedly. Cass saw Ira Bream with young Arch Cummings and a few other men, whom he took to be Slash M hands. Bream was smoking another cigarette. Cummings stared at Cass, the cold hostility in his face as usual.

"Come and get it," Cass said, and the big puncher wasted no time.

He came in with a rush and Cass hit him a short, jolting blow on the side of the jaw with his left hand. He didn't know how tough this puncher was, but he had to whip him. If he lost, he lost face as Ty Kincaid, the hard man.

The tall man steadied himself and came in at Cass, swinging wild, pulverizing punches. He was somewhat taller than Cass and a little heavier, but it was not a bad match, Cass himself being tall.

Stepping back, Cass eluded most of the punches, and then he moved in when the puncher eased up a little. His punches were shorter, more accurate, and he got his shoulder behind them. Twice he hit the puncher in the face, and then he shifted his attack and sank his right into the man's stomach.

The puncher had had a few drinks tonight, but Cass had had none, and that blow to the stomach did a lot of damage. Griff Munson's fighter bent over a little as he came in now, not anxious to take any more down there, and he was panting. Blood trickled from his mouth, and he had a cut under his right eye.

Cass had not come through unmarked, however. His lips were bruised, and he had a lump under his left eye. He'd been hit a dozen times on the arms and shoulders, and his arms were beginning to feel as if lead weights were attached to them.

The puncher lunged in, aiming another terrific blow at Cass's face. Cass pulled his head out of the way and cuffed the big man on the cheek with his left hand. He hit again, savagely this time, with his right, and then he drove the puncher before him with a fusillade of lefts and rights, driving him to his knees.

He hoped it was over, then, but the tall man had plenty of courage. With the crowd watching rather silently now, he got up and came in, shaking his head like a dog. He managed to back Cass against the wall of the building, but he didn't have enough strength to do anything when he got him there.

Cass tore away, anxious to finish it now. He struck out hard, driving his man before him, the sound of his punches like rocks being slammed into mud.

The tall puncher collapsed very suddenly. It wasn't any one particular punch which did it, but the accumulation of many. He went down on his knees again, staggered to his feet, and then pitched forward on his face without being hit. Cass had to step aside to avoid him as he fell.

He stood there for a few moments, feeling the pain in his arms, in his bruised, battered hands, and then a man said to him, "There's a bucket of water in the shed over there, mister, if you want to wash up."

The crowd was beginning to disperse as Cass

picked his way through them to the shed. Several buckboards were in under the shed, the horses unharnessed. He found the bucket of water in the light of a lantern hanging from a hook in the roof. The water had evidently been brought for the horses.

Taking off his shirt, Cass plunged his face and hands into the cool water. He kept his face under the water for a few moments, hoping that it would take away some of the swelling over his eye. He was not going to be a pretty sight when he went back to Katie McCoy, and he didn't like that.

He was dabbing at his face with his moistened handkerchief when Ira Bream sauntered in, the cigarette half-smoked now. The Slash M ramrod said, "You'll have some tough ones in every town, Kincaid, but you can handle yourself."

Cass looked at him. He said evenly, "Weren't you sure, Bream?"

Ira Bream looked at him uneasily. "What do you mean, Kincaid?"

"I don't like anybody who will set a dog on me," Cass told him tersely, "and the next time it happens I'll know damned well whose dog it is."

"Don't know what you're talkin' about," Bream scowled, but he was uneasy. He deftly changed the subject by saying, "At least you showed some o' them farmers around here that you can be tough, Kincaid."

Cass just looked at him, a contemptuous smile

on his face. He walked away after drying his face. The music had started up in the dance hall again, and he found Katie McCoy standing alone, evidently waiting for him.

She looked at him closely as he came up, and although he didn't feel like dancing now after using up all his energy on the tall puncher, he said, "That music sounds good."

She went out on the floor with him, and she said, "I heard there was a fight."

"A good one," Cass nodded. "Behind the dance hall."

"Were you in it?" Katie asked bluntly.

Cass smiled a little, and when he smiled his puffed lips hurt. He said, "I was pretty close to it."

Katie McCoy sniffed. "It must have been a good one if a bystander came out of it with an eye like that. We'll leave after this dance. You can hardly drag yourself around."

"All right with me," Cass grinned. "That was a hard fight to watch."

They didn't say any more about the fight until they were riding out of town. It was a little past midnight now, and other buckboards were leaving also, some of them with children sleeping in the back on piles of hay.

As they started up the grade, Katie said, "I'd like to know what you were fighting about."

Cass frowned and stared at the ears of the horses ahead of him. He said, "One of those things. Those boys were drinking a little too much. They got careless with their remarks."

"About me?" Katie asked quietly.

"About me," Cass lied.

She didn't say anything for a while, but he knew that she didn't believe him. They rode on in silence, and then Katie said, "You're a fool to fight for me, Mr. Kincaid."

"Am I?" Cass asked.

"I'll fight my own battles," Katie told him. "I always have."

Cass looked up at the sky. "You haven't always won them," he pointed out.

Katie McCoy turned to look at him. "How do you know?" she asked.

They were turning into the Wood Creek road now, and they weren't too far from her house. Cass shifted on the seat a little. He said, "A man can tell those things."

"I'll win, eventually," Katie said, and there was a deadly coldness in her voice which Cass Lorimer did not understand. There were many, many things about this girl with the copper-colored hair that he did not understand, and he didn't like it. Tonight, he'd had a fight over her, Griff Munson's girl, and he was sure she would bring him trouble if he had any contact with her.

He told himself that he was a fool even to have gone out with her tonight, and he tried to alleviate this self-condemnation with the thought that being Munson's lady friend she might possibly know something about the killing of Jeff. He couldn't mention Jeff as yet because he did not know where she stood with Munson. He had to know that before he committed himself.

They were coming up to the house now, and it was dark inside, indicating that the Indian woman had gone to bed. Cass stopped the chestnuts. He said, "Glad you came tonight?"

"I had a nice time," Katie told him, "and thank you."

She was evidently waiting for him to get off the seat and help her to the ground. Instead of getting down, Cass took her chin in his hand, turned her face around, and kissed her.

There was no response. She just sat there, waiting until he released her, and then she said quietly, "And what was that for?"

Cass scowled. He was staring at the horses' ears again, and he said a little gruffly, "Thought I'd find something out."

"Did you?" Katie asked him. She sat very straight, her hands folded in her lap, not looking at him.

"Where do you stand with Griff Munson?" Cass asked her flatly.

There was no hesitation on her part. The answer was prompt, cold, almost bitter, utterly confusing to Cass Lorimer. "I intend to marry him," Katie said.

Cass stepped down from the seat and came around to the other side of the buckboard. He didn't say anything as he waited for her to step down, giving her his hand. Katie McCoy said to him tersely, "What about it?"

Cass shrugged. "Your privilege," he murmured. He tried to keep the disappointment out of his voice, but it was there.

Katie McCoy stepped down from the seat. It was quite dark here because there were trees in front of the moon. He could not see her face clearly. She said, "I suppose you won't be around again?"

"Reckon not," Cass told her, and he was thinking that it was a strange question.

"All right," Katie nodded, and her voice seemed to be oddly dull now, the coldness gone out of it. She turned and walked toward the house.

Cass swung the chestnuts around and drove back to Red Rock. Farrel, the fat man, was pitching hay to some new horses which had just come in for the night. He came to the stable door when Cass drove up with the buckboard, and he stood there, scratching his fleshy face, watching Cass. When Cass stepped to the ground, he said, "Reckon you was right, mister."

"About what?" Cass asked absently.

"About who Griff Munson was bringin' to the dance tonight," the fat man told him.

Cass paid for the hire of the buckboard. He

didn't make any comment, and Farrel said, "Quite a fight that was too. I saw it."

Cass put his money folder away. He said, "Who was I fighting?"

"Bud Horner," Farrel told him. "Double Tree."

"He all right?" Cass asked indifferently. He was starting to turn away when the fat man's answer caught him up abruptly.

"He's dead."

Cass stared at the man. "Dead?" he repeated.

"Somebody shot him up other side o' town," Farrel stated, watching Cass's face closely for the reaction. "Shot him right off his horse as he was ridin' out tonight."

Cass said slowly, "When did this happen, mister?"

"Little after midnight," Farrel told him. "Matt Quinn's makin' an investigation. Reckon he'll want to talk to you, seein' as how you'd had a little trouble with Horner tonight."

Cass nodded. He turned and walked out of the alley to the street, a little dazed at this turn of events. There was the possibility that Bud Horner had had enemies, and one of them had shot him down. There was the other possibility that Horner had threatened to reveal who'd paid him to pick his fight with Kincaid, and he'd been silenced before his remarks could cause any embarrassment. Maybe Griff Munson didn't like to be embarrassed!

Chapter Seven

Matt Quinn was sitting in a wicker chair in the lobby of the Yankee House when Cass came through the door. Quinn had a half-smoked cigar in his mouth, and the cigar was dead. He sat alone, facing the door, his hat pushed back on his head.

Cass walked straight over to him, and he said, "You want to see me, Sheriff?"

Quinn looked at another chair nearby. He said, "Have a seat, Kincaid."

Cass sat down. "Heard there was a little trouble in town tonight," he began.

"Who told you?" Matt Quinn asked idly.

"Man at the Ace High Livery," Cass explained. "You want to see me about it?"

"Just a few questions," Quinn told him, shifting his cigar in his mouth and looking across the empty lobby. "You ever meet this Bud Horner before?"

"No," Cass said.

"You know any reason why anybody should want to kill him?"

"No," Cass said again.

Matt Quinn sighed. "Hell," he murmured, "we ain't gettin' anywhere. When did you leave town tonight?"

"About midnight," Cass told him. "Maybe a little later."

"With Miss McCoy?" Quinn wanted to know.

Cass nodded.

"You drive straight home?" Quinn asked him.

Cass smiled coldly. "She'll tell you when you ride out there tomorrow morning, Sheriff."

Matt Quinn smiled, too. "Maybe I won't ride out," he stated. "Maybe I'll take your word for it, Kincaid."

"Suit yourself," Cass told him. "Any more questions?"

Quinn stood up. "Can I buy you a drink?" he smiled.

Cass followed him into the hotel barroom which adjoined the lobby. The room was fairly well filled, and some of the drinkers turned to look at them as they came in.

Ira Bream and Arch Cummings were at the far end of the bar, and young Cummings had been leaning on the wood, a half-empty glass in his hand, facing the door from the lobby. He'd been drinking heavily, and his face was flushed.

There was something else about the yellow-haired tough which Cass noticed immediately. There was an extra color in Arch's face because of the drink, and his green eyes were wild, too, wild and—triumphant!

Cass turned his eyes away from the young Slash M rider, not wanting Arch Cummings to see the bitter contempt in them. Cummings, for quite some time, had wanted to kill a man. He'd bent all his efforts, feverishly, in that direction, and tonight his dream had been consummated—at the expense of big Bud Horner, who had fought well with his fists.

Horner had been killed from ambush, shot from his horse without a chance to draw his gun. It had been a loathsome murder, and yet Arch Cummings was rejoicing in it, possibly thinking of the day, too, when his gun would blast the hated Kincaid into oblivion.

Matt Quinn was saying, "A nice affair tonight, wasn't it?"

He poured two drinks from the bottle the bartender set before them. Cass said, "Who do you think shot Horner?"

Quinn stared at the glass in front of him, and then he shook his head. "Reckon somebody didn't like him. That's sure," he said.

"I liked him," Cass observed. "He didn't quit."

Matt Quinn nodded soberly. He didn't make any more comments, and Cass respected him for that. He didn't ask what the fight had been about, making it embarrassing.

Bream and Arch Cummings left a few minutes before Cass went up to his room. He took off his boots and in deep thought sat on the edge of the bed for some time. He'd accomplished exactly nothing tonight by going out with Katie McCoy.

Very possibly he had been the indirect cause of a man's death, and this thought was not a pleasant one. Tomorrow he had to be about his business. He had to get that over with. Katie McCoy and Valerie Schuyler could wait. It was very evident, though, that Katie was not waiting for *him.*

In the morning Cass saddled the buckskin and rode south out of Red Rock. Hilary Manville, the lawyer, watched him from his office window as he rode by, but Cass didn't even bother to notice him. He was supposed to talk with Manville about the Wood Creek homesteaders, but even though he was headed toward Wood Creek now he didn't bother to consult with the lawyer.

Turning off the stage road he made a wide circuit to avoid Katie McCoy's place, not particularly anxious to meet her this morning. He was on Slash M range again, passing plenty of Slash M stock. In the short circle he made here, he passed three abandoned homesteads, one hundred and sixty acre tracts, the few miserable little shanties fallen in. A coyote jumped out of one of them and raced across the open plains.

He hit the trickle of water which was Wood Creek about two miles west of Katie McCoy's place, and the first homesteader's shack he came to was along the course of the water. It was a nice location, a bit of cultivated ground behind the house, a field of hay badly burned now by the lack of rain, good grazing ground beyond.

The boy Cass had seen on the buckboard the other day was chopping wood in front of a lean-to in which the old gray horse stood, swishing her tail. The battered buckboard was pulled up alongside the lean-to.

The boy put down the ax when he heard Cass's horse, and he straightened up. He had dark hair, dark eyes and he was thin, probably ten or eleven years old, Cass figured, and suspicion and dislike were in his eyes, probably born there. That was the way the homesteader looked at the mounted man who ran his stock around, and sometimes over, the pitiful island of one hundred and sixty acres which was his kingdom.

Cass said, "What's your name, boy?"

He leaned forward, rubbing the saddle horn with his hands. The boy's clothes were in bad shape. His Levi's were so faded that it was hard to distinguish the color. They were patched, and patched poorly too. He wore a shirt which had probably belonged to his father, and this, too, was badly worn. The shoes on his feet were falling to pieces. He was thin and didn't look too strong. There was a delicateness about him which Cass did not usually associate with the scrawny, hard-bitten nester children.

The boy didn't answer immediately. He glanced toward the shack from which a thin curl of wood smoke lifted into the brassy sky. Then he said, "Louis."

"This your homestead, Louis?" Cass asked him.

"Reckon I'll answer the questions, mister," a dry voice came from the open doorway.

Cass saw the gray-haired man standing there, his rifle in his hand again. He had big, gnarled hands, but he was not a big man. His shoulders were bent is if he'd followed a plow all of his life, and there were deep lines in his face. He watched Cass steadily through a pair of faded blue eyes in which there was no warmth.

Cass said to him, "You won't need that rifle, friend."

"I know better than you what I need in this country, mister," the gray-haired man observed.

The boy, Louis, shifted uneasily. He looked at Cass, at the buckskin, the admiration in his eyes for the horse. Cass said, "You have a nice piece of property here. Prove it yet?"

"My business," the homesteader told him. "Why?"

Cass shrugged and smiled. "Maybe I'd like to buy it," he said.

"It ain't for sale," the man told him quietly. "You can tell Griff Munson that."

Cass started to roll a cigarette, and he watched the gray-haired man as he moistened the paper with his tongue. He said, "Who says I work for Munson?"

"Everybody works for Munson," the man scowled, "one way or another."

Cass went off in a new tack. As he lit the cigarette he said, "I'm the fellow who took Munson's girl to the dance last night. That sound like I work for Munson?"

He was fairly sure the homesteader had heard about that. In a country starved for news, an incident like that would have made a big splash.

The homesteader was staring at him, thoughtfully, as if trying to figure out some reason why Cass should lie about this.

"You the feller had the fight with that rider from Double Tree?" he said finally.

"That's right," Cass nodded. "Kincaid."

The nester seemed mollified. He leaned the rifle against the doorsill and he came forward. He said gruffly, "Morse Claybank. My nephew, Louis. What can I do for you, Kincaid?"

Cass looked around. "Just the two of you?" he asked, surprised.

Claybank nodded. "My wife died three years ago," he said, his eyes clouding a little. "Louis' folks were dead when he was a baby. I'm bringin' him up."

Cass slid from the saddle. He tossed the reins to Louis and he said, "Give him some water—not too much." He saw the delight in the boy's eyes. To the uncle he said, "I could stand a cup of coffee, Claybank, if you're not short."

"Never short for a man who'll stand up against Griff Munson," Claybank said tersely. "Come on inside."

The interior was about what Cass had expected. There were two rooms, the kitchen being little more than a shed in the rear. Morse Claybank had evidently been doing the best he knew how under the circumstances, but the circumstances were a little too much for him. There was very little in the way of furniture, and Claybank had constructed everything himself, crude bunks, table, a few chairs. The windows had oilcloth tacked across them. The floor was hard-packed dirt.

The coffeepot was on the stove, and the nester poured Cass a cup as he sat down at the table. The coffee was weak, indicating that Claybank was short of this staple, and using more water than was required to make a good pot.

Cass said to him, "You prove up on your land, Claybank?"

The nester rubbed his jaw. "Had it two years," he said. "Scraped up enough money to pay the government. I own it now."

"You don't want to sell," Cass said.

Morse Claybank looked at him. "Munson offered to buy me out," he said, "for about one quarter what I'm worth. I told him to go to hell with himself. He offered plenty more, an' I still told him to go to hell."

"That why you carry a rifle with you now?" Cass smiled.

Claybank laughed mirthlessly. "I remember what happened to Jeff Lorimer," he said.

Cass had been stirring his coffee aimlessly. He stopped now, and he stared at the table.

"What happened to Lorimer?" he asked.

"Had a homestead up the creek," Claybank said bitterly. "Good water, a nice piece o' land. Munson wanted it, an' Lorimer wouldn't sell. He was shot down in front of his house one night."

"Munson?" Cass asked, his voice emotionless.

Claybank shrugged. "Munson was behind it," he stated, "but there ain't anybody kin prove it."

Cass said, "You weren't nearby when it happened?"

The homesteader looked at him. "Lorimer's wife came over here with the little girl after it happened. Reckon I was their nearest neighbor. I drove her in to see Sheriff McElroy, but McElroy was Munson's man. I didn't know that, then. He looked around, said he'd do what he could, an' did nothin'. It was Munson or one of his boys who shot Lorimer down."

Cass nodded. He sipped his coffee, knowing that he'd come up against another blank wall here. The man who'd shot Jeff was evidently known only to Munson or his associates. The next step, then, was to strike up a friendship with one of Munson's riders.

"You figurin' on buyin' in this part o' the country?" Claybank asked curiously.

Cass shrugged. "Hard to say," he stated. "I'm looking around."

"You run cattle on this range," Claybank told him, "an' you buck Griff Munson."

Cass said, "Why does Munson want these homesteads up on the creek?"

"Good water," Claybank said promptly, "good grazin' land, an' all them big ranchers are pigs. They never git enough."

Cass nodded. Claybank didn't know. None of them up here apparently knew the reason for Munson's intense interest in the creek property.

Outside, the boy, Louis, came up with the horse, and he was stroking the buckskin's nose.

"Like him?" Cass asked.

"Yes, sir," Louis smiled. He was an unusual boy, and Cass liked him immediately. He seemed to have a lot more breeding than the ordinary nester boy would have.

Riding off, Cass left the two watching him from the lean-to. He continued due south now, following the course of the creek. It was less than a dozen yards across, a gravelly bottom, good water, but nothing exceptional about it. Cass frowned as he rode the buckskin along the sandy bank.

He passed three more homesteads, wretched places, but with plenty of water they might eventually make out here. He had a pretty good idea why they'd turned down Munson's offer to buy, even after he'd raised the price. These nesters were thick-skulled farmers and they didn't like to be pushed around; they didn't like Munson, either, and they would refuse to sell to him even if they realized that they couldn't make a go of it along the creek.

Slash M was south and east of the creek, and after passing the last shack, Cass turned the buckskin in that direction. It was a little after high noon when he spotted the big sprawling ranch house from the top of a grade.

It was not a single building, but a clump of buildings, almost a small town in size. The main structure was L-shaped, one story high, containing at least a dozen rooms. There were other buildings, a long, low bunkhouse, barns, sheds, a number of corrals.

Cass sat on the buckskin staring down at the spread, and the bitter thought was running through him. *Down there was Jeff Lorimer's little wealth, too.*

He rode in, dismounting near one of the corrals, and a rider came out of the stable close by to look at him. He was a short, chunky man with the beginnings of a paunch. His belt buckle held his stomach in. In his mouth was a half-smoked cigar, and he carried a blacksmith's hammer in his hand. Cass had heard the hammering when he rode down the slope. He said now, "Munson around?"

The Slash M man wrinkled his stub nose. He had a pair of smoky blue eyes and he needed a shave. "*Mister* Munson," he scowled.

Cass looked at him and said coolly, "Hell with you." He added, "I'm Kincaid."

It had the desired effect. The stubby man's mouth opened and the cigar nearly fell out. He gulped, "Sure—sure, Kincaid. Griff's gone to town. Expect him back any minute."

Cass tied the buckskin to the corral. He said with his back turned, "What do they call you?"

"Stub Moran," the short rider murmured. "If you ain't et, Kincaid, I'll have the cook rustle up some grub for you."

"Go ahead," Cass told him.

As Stub Moran hustled off, the cigar puffing in his mouth, Cass wondered if he would be the one to eventually confide in. He walked past the stable, examining the layout, eventually coming closer to the main house. He noticed that there was a little flower garden inside the L, and this was surprising. Munson was a cattle man, and a big one. He probably wouldn't bother much with flowers, but there were flowers here. The little plat was well watered, and sheltered somewhat from the hot sun by a trellis.

Coming up to the low porch, Cass eased himself into the shade and sat down on the steps.

There still had been no break in the weather. The sky was blue and cloudless, and the sun at this hour scorching.

From his position on the porch he could see two riders bringing in a band of about two dozen horses—Morgans—and Cass watched them as they turned the fine animals into an enclosure down near the south pasture. Griff Munson had everything—stock, land, Morgan horses and even a woman who wanted to marry him. The thought of Katie McCoy brought a frown to Cass's face.

He heard a strange sound from within the house, and he had to listen carefully for a moment to identify it. It was the sound of rolling wheels, small wheels. Then the screen door was kicked open and a wheelchair came out, bouncing over the step.

Cass got up, trying to conceal the surprise in his eyes. A girl sat in the wheelchair, a young girl, probably no older than Katie McCoy. She had golden hair, and the brightest blue eyes Cass had ever seen. She was frail like a China doll, but the smile on her face was warm and fine.

Taking off his hat, Cass said quickly, "I didn't know any one was at home. Heard Griff was in town."

"I'm Griff's sister, Nina," the girl told him. "Please sit down."

A little dazed, Cass sat down on the step again. "Didn't know Griff had a sister. I'm Kincaid."

The name meant nothing to her, and he hadn't thought that it would. Nina said, "Griff should be back any minute now, Mr. Kincaid. Are you a new man with the outfit?"

"Reckon you'd call it that, ma'am," Cass told her. He didn't like this now. He didn't like the thought of Munson having a sister, and he wondered why Katie McCoy hadn't mentioned that to him. Then he remembered that they'd said practically nothing about Griff Munson while they were together.

"Do you think we'll ever have any rain, Mr. Kincaid?" Nina frowned, looking up at the sky. "This hot spell is just about ruining my garden."

"I thought it looked very nice," Cass told her.

"You should see it," Nina gushed, "after a good rainstorm."

Stub Moran came around the corner of the building, took off his hat, and said, "Your grub's ready, if you want to eat, Mr. Kincaid."

Cass got up again. "Reckon I will," he said. "Glad to meet you, Miss Munson."

He went off with Stub, and he was sure Nina was sorry to see him go. She was lonely out here, and there weren't too many people to talk to. Cass said to Stub as they walked toward the cook's shack, "Didn't know Munson had a sister. How long she been out here?"

"Griff brought her out two years ago," Stub

explained. "Treats her like a queen. The best ain't good enough fer Nina Munson."

"That right," Cass murmured.

He went into the cook shack, and the cook slapped a big steak down on his platter and filled his cup with coffee. He was mumbling something about some damned sidewinders comin' in every five minutes fer food.

Cass didn't say anything, understanding the temperaments of bunkhouse cooks. Stub Moran sat across the table from him, every once in a while his eyes straying to Cass's gun on his hip. The little man said finally, "Heard about you down in El Paso, Kincaid."

Cass nodded and went on eating. He understood this—the hero worship of a man who, too, would have liked to be a famous killer but lacked the nerve and the skill. He was beginning to think that Stub might be the man, and he slipped a cigar from his vest pocket and rolled it across the table to the short man.

Stub Moran's eyes lighted up. "Much obliged, Kincaid," he murmured. He picked up the cigar, smelled it, and said, "That time you shot Ace Bartley in Galeyville. Feller over in Travis City told me about that."

He was fishing here for details, gory details, but Cass went on eating coolly, drinking his coffee.

"Was that Bartley pretty fast?" Stub asked.

Cass looked up from his plate. "We'll have a

drink in town some day," he stated. "I'll tell you about it then."

Stub Moran beamed. "Sure," he nodded. "Sure, Mr. Kincaid."

They heard a horse moving by outside, and Moran got up and crossed to the door. He called back, "Might be Griff Munson now."

It was Munson and he came in a few moments later as Cass was finishing his coffee. He came over and sat down on the other side of the table where Moran had been sitting. He was immaculately dressed as usual, clean white shirt and black tie, expensive black coat and Stetson, cleanly shaven.

"How are you, Kincaid?" he asked.

"Thought I'd drop in," Cass told him. "Just come from Wood Creek."

Griff Munson nodded. He was smiling pleasantly, drumming with his strong fingers on the table. Cass thought about Jeff Lorimer, and then about Nina Munson. He didn't like it.

"They won't sell," Cass said. "They like their land over there on Wood Creek."

Munson laughed gayly. "That right?" he asked.

"Spoke to a man named Claybank," Cass went on idly. "He seems like the tough one."

"He's the one we'll have to soften, then," Munson chuckled. There was no malice in his voice, no ill feeling toward Cass for going out with Katie McCoy the previous evening. He was congenial as usual, very smooth, a bland smile on his face. It was almost as if he were laughing inwardly at some huge joke.

Cass said, "I had to look around first. There's plenty of time to get rough."

Griff Munson nodded. "You know your business," he said. "When you're ready, see Manville."

"I will," Cass told him.

Munson got up and sauntered toward the door. He said, "You meet my sister?"

"Met her," Cass nodded. "Surprised you had a sister."

Griff Munson put one hand on the doorframe. Cass noticed the gold ring on the finger, the clean nails. Munson said, "Have a little surprise for you, too, Kincaid."

Cass looked at him. He saw the humor lurking deep down in Griff Munson's turquoise-colored eyes.

"Just received a wire," Munson said, "from your brother."

Cass's eyes flicked. He moistened his lips. "That right?" he asked.

"Your brother, Asa," Griff Munson said.

Cass looked at him. "Reckon I know his name," he said evenly.

Munson grinned. "He'll be in on the stage in about a week," he stated. "Thought you'd like to know."

Cass took a cigar from his vest pocket and bit off the end. He put the cigar in his mouth, and then said around it, "That's good news."

He sat there when Griff Munson went out. He could hear the cook banging dishes in the next room, cursing occasionally. He repeated to himself, *Good news.* He wasn't smiling, though.

Chapter Eight

It was three o'clock in the afternoon when Cass left Slash M. Stepping into the saddle down near the corral, he saw Nina and Griff Munson sitting on the porch, and Nina waved a hand to him. He waved back, and he noticed that Griff was staring at him intently.

Stub Moran came out of the barn, face sweaty, dirt-streaked. The little rider said, "See you in town sometime, Mr. Kincaid."

"Why not?" Cass murmured. Moran had half of the cigar butt in his mouth, and he was grinning, a little proud that he'd struck up a friendship with an illustrious killer.

Crossing a meadow, Cass picked up the trace which led back to the stage road. He rode slowly, deep in thought. According to Griff Munson, Kincaid's brother, Asa, was coming to Red Rock in a week or so, which meant that he had one week to find Jeff's killer and settle his business here. If Asa turned up before that time, Griff Munson would set his hired hands after Cass Lorimer the way a rancher set his pack of dogs after a lobo wolf. He knew he wouldn't stand a chance against those odds.

He found himself wondering about this sudden visit of Ty Kincaid's brother. In their first meeting in the back room of the Plains Saloon, Munson had made no mention of the fact that brother Asa was coming to Red Rock, and this was a little unusual. Asa, undoubtedly, was another hired gunhand like his brother, and it seemed illogical that Munson had not asked about him when they'd met. There was the possibility, of course, that Griff Munson had been having separate negotiations with brother Asa in a different part of the country, and he was springing Asa's coming as a pleasant surprise.

Cass fumbled with his shirt pocket for his tobacco pouch, slipped it out, and then as he was undoing the strings the pouch dropped from his fingers. He had to reach down suddenly, bending his head and the upper part of his body, to snatch at the pouch before it fell to the ground, and as he did so a rifle cracked from the stand of timber a hundred yards up the slope on his right.

He heard the whine of the bullet as it passed very close to his head, and even as he slid from the saddle in one easy motion, putting the buckskin between himself and the rifleman, he made a mental note of the fact that the bushwhacker in the timber was using a Winchester .73. He'd heard that sound before.

The nearest shelter was a clump of low rocks about a dozen yards up along the trace. Cass sprinted for it, making the nearest rocks in a long dive just as the Winchester snarled again.

The slug kicked up dirt a few feet to the rear.

Gun in hand, he crouched behind the rocks, his face tense, the bitterness raging through him. He'd been fired on from ambush, a deliberate murder attempt with a high velocity rifle, and the killer was still hidden up there among the trees, his Winchester lined on this clump of rock, waiting for him to make a move.

Armed only with a six-gun he was at a great disadvantage here. At that distance the killer could pick him off easily the moment he showed himself, while he could not hope to do too much damage with a short arm. He noticed with some small surprise that he still had the tobacco pouch clutched in his left hand. That sudden movement to retrieve the falling pouch had very possibly saved his life.

He lay there on his side, completely hidden behind the sheltering rocks, and he made his smoke, lighting it, puffing on the cigarette for a while, the Colt gun resting on a slab of rock in front of him. There was a hundred yards of open space between the stand of timber and the trace, and a killer who shot from ambush wouldn't cross that space in a thousand years.

The buckskin had moved on a few rods and was waiting in the slight shade of a ledge up the trace. The sun was scorchingly hot against the rocks here, and Cass cursed softly as he picked up the gun, feeling the heat of the hot metal.

He had a fairly good idea who the killer was up in the timber. There was one man in Red Rock who hated him, who'd been insulted and shamed by him. Arch Cummings had shot one man from ambush, and he'd probably discovered that it was easy. He was at it again.

Cass took off his hat, perched it on the barrel of his gun, and lifted the hat above the edge of the rock. The Winchester cracked again, and the slug ricocheted off the rock a few inches below the protruding hat. Pulling the hat down hastily, Cass put it on. He fired twice in the general direction of the marksman, and then he crawled the few yards to the far edge of the rock out-cropping, slipped the hat off again, and peeped carefully around the edge of the rock.

Powder smoke drifted up above the trees from a thick clump of pine. Cass sent two shots in among the trees, knowing full well that if Cummings were concealed there, he would be down low, well-protected behind a fallen log. The shots were meant to worry him, to let him know that he was in a gun fight.

Cass sent another shot at the clump of pine, and then pulled back to reload. The Winchester spat again, and the slug passed harmlessly over his head. He lay there, listening carefully, and then he thought he heard a horse moving away at a fast pace beyond the stand of timber.

When he lifted his hat again on the end of the

gun barrel there was no answering shot from the rifle. Scrambling up then, he made a break for the buckskin over at the ledge, wondering as he ran if that Winchester would spit death at him again.

Nothing happened. In the saddle he bolted for the protection of the timber, moving up the slope several hundred yards below the spot from which the shots had come. It was cool here after the terrible heat of the open rocks below. A foot-deep bed of pine needles cushioned the hoofbeats of the buckskin. He moved gradually up toward the ambush, and then when he saw the trees thin out at his left, he rode out of the timber and discovered the fresh hoofprints heading north toward Red Rock.

It was too late now to pursue the man. By this time he would be back on the stage road, and if he rode in to Red Rock it would be impossible to pick him out as the bushwhacker.

Dismounting, Cass walked back through the trees, backtracking on the lone horse and rider. He discovered the spot where the animal had been tied, and there were droppings. The ground was scuffed here, indicating that the horse had been tied for some time while the rider waited in the timber below, watching the trace.

His jaw hard, Cass moved on through the timber. Fifty yards below he discovered the huge fallen pine, the lightning marks high up on its trunk. Down in the hollow left, where the roots had been ripped up, he noticed several small shining objects—rifle cartridge shells. He saw the heelprints in the soft earth where the rifleman had crouched, his Winchester lined on the target below. There was even a thick root stretched horizontally in front of the spot where the man had lain, and he could have rested his rifle on that root, steadying it as he took aim and fired his shot.

Walking back through the trees, Cass Lorimer had to reflect on the sober thought that someone was very anxious to kill him—so anxious that he'd waited here in the timber, possibly for several hours, knowing that Cass Lorimer had left Red Rock that morning, and might very possibly come back along this trace.

If one attempt had been made, another would follow, and another. If the attempted killer were the despicable Arch Cummings, the yellow-haired Slash M rider could move around at will, biding his time, sending that fatal shot from a back alley some night, or waiting again in the brush, his Winchester following the target.

Cass rode the buckskin back to the trace, followed it to the stage road, and came in to Red Rock after four in the afternoon. As he moved down the grade into town the heat became more oppressive. The sun wouldn't go down for another three hours, and there was still plenty of heat in it. He could feel it on his left side as he moved into Main Street.

There were no horses at the tie racks along the street. A man who let a horse stand in that terrific heat was not a man. Any recent riders coming into town would have taken their mounts into a livery or left them in one of the shady alleys along the street.

Any rider, too, who had been laying out in the brush for several hours, even in the shade, and then had ridden pretty fast into Red Rock, would be mighty thirsty, and a cool glass of beer would go good.

Thinking of this, Cass pulled up at the first saloon, the Ox Horn. He looked in over the bat-wing doors. The bar was empty. Even the bartender was out of sight for the moment, and an old man with a broom swished idly at the sawdust on the floor.

Cass passed on to the Pleasant Hour Saloon, and then the Bushwhacker, an appropriate name for the occasion, but only in the Pleasant Hour did he find any patrons, and these sat at a card table in a corner. From the looks of them they'd been there a long time, and they were townsmen.

The Plains Saloon was next on this side of the street, and as Cass came up to it, Sheriff Quinn moved across the road from the Yankee House. He'd evidently been sitting in the shade of the porch.

Stepping up on the boardwalk, Quinn nodded. Cass waited for him outside the doors of the saloon, the sudden thought coming to him that if Quinn had been sitting on that porch for any length of time he'd have seen a rider coming in.

Quinn said casually, "Lookin' for somebody, Kincaid?"

"I might be," Cass nodded.

"Who?" Quinn asked.

"You see anybody ride in here the past thirty minutes?" Cass countered.

Matt Quinn's flinty eyes flicked. He leaned his weight against one of the porch pillars, and he studied Cass thoughtfully. His answer was quite surprising. He said, "Ira Bream."

Cass moistened his lips. He looked in over the doors of the saloon. There were several men at the big bar here—two riders he didn't recognize, and a drummer, one of the men he'd seen on the Yankee House porch. Neither Bream nor Arch Cummings were in the saloon.

"What's up?" Quinn wanted to know.

"Bream ride in from the south?" Cass asked him.

Matt Quinn's thin lips curved a little in a smile. He said, "You have your questions, mister, but no answers. Bream came down the stage road from the north. Might have been up to Windham. Griff Munson buys his hay up there sometimes."

Cass nodded. He said briefly, "I could stand

a glass of cold beer, Sheriff. Someone threw a few shots at me from the timber along the Slash M trace. He rode this way after he got tired of playing."

He went into the saloon, then, Quinn following him, rubbing his jaw. Cass looked at him in the bar mirror, waiting for the questions.

Quinn said, "Who would want to shoot you from the brush, Kincaid?"

"Maybe," Cass observed, "the same hombre who shot Bud Horner the other night."

"Doc Palmer took a Winchester rifle ball from Horner's back," Quinn stated. "Bullet passed right through the heart, lodged underneath the backbone."

Cass nodded. He drank his beer when the bartender brought it, and he wondered about Bream, and about Matt Quinn. According to Quinn no one else had ridden into Red Rock besides Bream, and Bream had come in from the north, which eliminated him, unless Bream had circled to swing in from the north, thus fooling anyone who may have watched him. Also, Quinn could be lying. Quinn could still be Griff Munson's man. He didn't know what lay behind those cool, flinty blue eyes.

"That a Winchester shootin' at you?" Quinn asked him.

Cass put the beer glass down. "It was," he stated.

Quinn grimaced. "Plenty o' Winchesters in this part of the country," he said.

"One too many for me," Cass told him thinly. "I figure on silencing that one pretty shortly."

"Luck," Quinn smiled. He lifted his glass.

Hilary Manville, the lawyer, came in through the doors. He'd evidently spotted Cass from his window. A broad, flat smile was on his gray face as he approached them.

"A warm afternoon, gentlemen," he grinned, showing his teeth.

Quinn nodded. He said to Cass, "Better walk easy, Kincaid." He left the saloon, then, and Manville pulled up at Cass's elbow. He said quickly, "Any news from up Wood Creek?"

Cass looked at him. He said, "I work for Griff Munson. I give him a report, and then only when I'm damned ready."

Hilary Manville smiled sheepishly. "I know," he agreed. "My business, though, is to contact these homesteaders after you have seen them. I have to know when the time is ripe."

"It's not ripe now," Cass informed him.

Hilary Manville frowned. "I see," he said.

"What's Munson want with that extra land?" Cass asked him. "I had a look at it today. The homesteaders can keep it for my part."

Manville shrugged. "You know these big ranchers," he explained. "Can't stand the sight of homesteaders. One brings another, and pretty soon the country's filled up. I'd say Munson's trying to discourage that."

Cass kept the bitterness out of his voice with an effort. He said casually, "He's doing pretty well so far." He'd found out what he wanted to know. Manville knew nothing about Wood Creek, either. He was just in it for the commission Munson would pay him to acquire the homesteads along the creek.

"He'll do better," Manville grinned. "I knew his father when he was out here years ago."

"What happened to him?" Cass wanted to know.

"Had political ambitions," Manville said. "Wanted to represent the territory in Washington when this state was still a territory. Guess he wasn't the man for politics. They made a monkey out of him. I heard he shot himself back east. Griff came out later to take over the ranch."

Cass digested these facts, understanding Munson a little better. Griff was hard and tough. He'd seen his father take a beating in life. He didn't intend to follow in his footsteps.

Outside, a few minutes later, Cass headed down the street to the little shed the artist, John Schuyler, had rented and in which he worked on some of his western paintings. The shed was in a back alley where it was fairly cool in contrast to Main Street, which was an inferno. At least in the narrow alleys a slight breeze seemed to be blowing.

When Cass hesitated in the doorway of the little building, John Schuyler called to him cheerily from the rear, "Come in, Kincaid."

Cass saw the drawings hanging on the walls, some of them only rough sketches, partly finished; others complete in all the details. There were a number of canvas paintings, too, all western scenes; a rider breaking a wild pony; riders bringing in horses; and sketches of cowpunchers—all very well done.

Taking a chair against the wall, Cass said, "You picked out the only cool spot in town, Schuyler."

The Englishman grinned. "I tried working in my room at the Yankee House for a while," he explained, "but the heat got me. In the daytime it's like being in an oven. When do you think this heat spell will be broken?"

Cass shrugged. "When it breaks," he observed, "it'll break hard. You'll see more water around here, mister, than you ever saw in your life."

"Valerie doesn't seem to mind it too much," Schuyler told him. "She's crazy about this part of the country. I guess it's the clear air and the sunsets, the wide open spaces."

Cass nodded. He wondered what Valerie Schuyler did with herself in the daytime when her brother was busy with his paintings. He wondered, too, how Matt Quinn would take it if he, Cass, were to ask her to go riding some time. And he wondered if she would go with him after he'd taken Katie McCoy to the dance.

That had been a mistake, and he knew that now. It had been a small boy stunt, defying Griff Munson, the big man of the territory, and it had accomplished exactly nothing. Indirectly, an innocent rider had been shot down.

Cass said, "Must be pretty dull for your sister in a small town like this."

John Schuyler laughed. "She loves to ride," he explained. "Wouldn't be surprised if she were out now."

Cass didn't know if that was a hint, or just a statement of fact. He made no comment on it, and after a while he drifted back to the Yankee House. He had his supper at six o'clock in the hotel dining room, eating alone, and he was finishing when Valerie Schuyler came in, alone, also.

Cass stood up, and she came to his table, smiling. She said, "I'm to meet John here at seven, but I suppose he's finishing up some work in his studio."

"Having my coffee," Cass invited. "Won't you sit down, ma'am?"

Valerie took the seat opposite him. Cass caught the faint odor again of violet perfume. She was in green this evening—a green silk dress with a white bow, rather out of place in a drab dining room like this, but Cass suspected that she didn't have too many opportunities to wear her better dresses in Red Rock, and she wore them just for the change.

He said, "Your brother tells me you do a lot of riding, Miss Schuyler."

Valerie nodded. "I go out nearly every day," she told him. "It's beautiful up in the hills. You don't really feel the heat until you get back to town."

Cass stirred his coffee, looking at it as he spoke. He said, "You'll have to show me some of those hills some morning, ma'am."

When he looked up she was smiling at him, and she said, "You name the day, Mr. Kincaid."

"Shouldn't rain tomorrow," Cass observed.

Valerie Schuyler's laugh tinkled. "I like your western way of putting things," she said. "Ten o'clock be all right?"

"Wait for you in the lobby," Cass nodded.

John Schuyler was coming in now, and Cass got up when Valerie left him to join her brother. He went up to his room for a few minutes, and he stood by the window which faced toward the north. It was time to open up to let in the night breeze.

The window opened on the porch roof on this side of the house. He was on the side street here and directly across the road was the blank wall of the barber shop. The shop was a one-story structure with a false front, and he was thinking as he stood at the window, looking out, how easy it would be for someone with a rifle—with a Winchester—to get up on that roof from the back of the building, and put a bullet through his window as he lighted the lamp when he came back that evening. The table and the lamp were close by the window, which meant that he'd have to stand directly in front of the window when he put the lamp on.

Before he went downstairs he moved the table and lamp over to a blank wall, and he examined the lock on the door. It was not much of a lock. One hard shove of a shoulder would break it, but he could always stand a chair against the doorknob, holding it until he could get a gun in his hand if he needed one.

He played cards that night with John Schuyler and two other town men until a little past midnight, a friendly game for low stakes. He sat facing the door this night, watching who came in. The only Slash M rider he recognized was Stub Moran. The little man wandered into the saloon, lifted a hand to Cass in greeting, grinned, and moved on to the bar.

Moran was still in the saloon when Cass stepped out of the game. The little Slash M rider joined him at the bar, and he said to Cass, grinning, "Must be pretty quiet in Red Rock for a chap like you, Kincaid."

Cass smiled. "Reckon I don't kill a man every evening, Stub," he said. "One or two a week is plenty."

Moran's grin broadened. He was being kidded and he knew it, but kidded by a great man, and it was a big thing in his life. He said, "Drink's on me, Mr. Kincaid."

Cass shook his head. "I promised you one," he murmured, and he signaled for the bartender.

He didn't get anything out of Moran that night, but he'd established the relationship, and that was sufficient for the time being. He'd learned that Moran had been with Slash M for two years. He'd been around when Cass's brother Jeff was killed.

Walking back to the Yankee House, Cass gave the alley a wide berth. He kept his hand on his gun as he went past them, and he walked out on the edge of the wooden boardwalk. The cooling breeze from the Estrellas was blowing now, driving the heat of the day out of this parched town, but it would be back tomorrow, and the day after.

Crossing the road, he entered the Yankee House. He noticed the clerk dozing at the desk. The lobby was empty at he went up the stairs, walked down the dimly-lighted corridor to his room, and pushed open the door.

Again he had his hand on his gun as he shoved the door in, and he stood to one side, letting the light from the corridor illuminate most of the little room. It was empty, and he stepped inside, closing the door behind him. Moving in the darkness toward the lamp on the other side of the room, he was feeling in his pockets for a match when he heard the slight noise outside on the porch roof. It was very slight, as if a boot had moved on the roof.

Chapter Nine

Standing by the lamp, Cass listened very carefully. He had his gun out of the holster now, and he'd swung around to face the window, very glad that he'd shut the door. The window was open, as he'd left it, the shade pulled down halfway. The shade had not been flapping, and that sound very definitely had come from outside the room—on the porch roof.

He hadn't thought of the porch roof before, and he wondered at that because from the porch roof a man could make very sure of his shot, and there was easy access to it. Crouching up there in the darkness along the side street he could not be seen from below, and he would be within five or six feet of his victim.

Right now he would be flattened against the wall to one side of the window, waiting for Cass to light the lamp, revealing his position in the room. Cass's long delay in striking the match was probably already causing him some worry.

The gun still in his hand, Cass felt around for the chair which had stood near the lamp table. He picked it up soundlessly and deposited it farther back in the room, approximately in the center of the room, facing the window.

Then he sat down slowly, making sure that the chair did not creak beneath his weight. He kept the gun trained on the window, and he sat very still. He sat for a full minute, and then another minute, knowing that the killer on the roof was sweating out there, wondering why he didn't light the lamp. He'd seen the door open and he knew Cass was in the room.

Five minutes passed, and Cass still sat motionless in the chair, his gun trained on the window. He was beginning to wonder if his sense of hearing had been correct when he noticed the darker shadow edging in from the left side of the window just below the shade.

Then he very clearly saw the gun barrel sliding soundlessly over the window sill. The shape of a man's head came into view, hatless, very blurry in the dim light.

Cass steadied his gun. He watched the barrel of that gun moving, and he could have easily put a bullet through the head of the man outside. At eight feet he could hardly miss. Instead he said softly, "This way, friend."

Then he dropped sideways to the floor as the gun flamed red and orange in the window, and the roar of it filled the room. He fired at the flash as he hit the floor, and then he fired again before scrambling to his feet and lunging for the window.

He went through in a long dive, scraping his right shoulder on the half-opened window, tearing the shirt. The porch roof was a dozen-feet wide, and he had plenty of room to roll when he landed on the outside without falling over the edge.

He had one brief glimpse of a man's head and shoulders disappearing over the edge of the roof at the rear of the building. His shot ripped into the rain gutter.

As he scrambled to his feet and raced toward the spot where the killer had climbed down, he could hear the man stumbling among tin cans and litter in the back lot behind the hotel. When he crouched on the porch roof he saw a horse racing out of the lot, swinging around the corner of a shed, the rider low in the saddle. He couldn't distinguish the rider, but he had a good look at the horse. It was a black and white spotted animal. He remembered that Arch Cummings had ridden such a horse the first day he'd met the young Slash M rider.

The flurry of shots had brought a crowd down to the corner, and they were staring up at him as he walked back along the porch roof to his window. He saw Matt Quinn's angular shape pushing through the crowd, and then Quinn headed for the door of the hotel.

Climbing back through the window, Cass felt his shoulder gingerly. His hand came away wet with blood. He lit the lamp, then, and poured a basin of water from the pitcher. Matt Quinn came through the door as he was stripping off the ripped shirt.

Quinn walked over to the window and looked out without a word. He said when he turned around, "That Winchester again?"

Cass smiled at him grimly as he started to bathe the blood from the bruised shoulder. He said, "I didn't see the gun, Sheriff."

"See the man?" Quinn wanted to know.

"Not to recognize him," Cass said.

Quinn shook his head. "Twice in one day," he murmured. "Reckon somebody don't like you mighty bad, Kincaid."

Cass just nodded. He took a clean shirt from the drawer, placed a handkerchief over the shoulder, adjusting it so that it rested against the shirt, and then buttoned the shirt.

Quinn said to him casually, "Kind o' late to be steppin' out tonight, Kincaid."

"Is it?" Cass said. He hung the torn shirt over the bed post and he walked toward the door. He could hear Quinn coming behind him, whistling tunelessly as he walked down the corridor and then down the stairs.

Outside, in the crowd gathered on the hotel porch, he found Stub Moran, and he took the little man by the arm, walking him down the street.

"That shot at you?" Moran wanted to know.

"Arch Cummings ride a black and white paint horse?" Cass asked him.

"Three white stockin's," Stub Moran nodded.

"Bought him from an Injun up in Windham. I was there."

Cass just nodded. He pushed on ahead of Moran and he turned down the alley of the hotel livery. Moran came down after him to watch him saddle the buckskin. The little Slash M rider stood there, rolling a cigarette, saying nothing for a while. He stated finally, "That Arch Cummings is one damn fool, Kincaid."

"He might be a dead fool before the night is up," Cass said tersely. He led the buckskin out of the stable and stepped into the saddle. Stub Moran watched him, jaw sagging, as he rode out of the alley.

A few minutes later Moran joined up with Cass on the stage road leading south out of Red Rock. Moran said abruptly, "Arch throw them shots at you, Kincaid?"

"I'll find out," Cass told him.

He rode on silently until they turned into the Slash M trace, and then he said to Moran, "Cummings in the bunkhouse with you boys?"

Moran spat and nodded. "Eighteen of us in the shack," he stated. "Allus some o' the boys out at the line camps, though."

Cass didn't say any more. Thirty minutes later they raised the lights of Slash M down across the meadow. There were lights in the main house, indicating that Griff Munson was still awake, or his sister.

"Munson in?" Cass asked.

"Hard to say," Moran told him. "He's in an' he's out." He was very vague, and Cass started to think bitterly of Katie McCoy again, wondering if Munson was spending many of his evenings down there. If she intended to marry him—

They crossed the meadow, stopping in front of the corral. Cass could make out the dim shapes of the horses inside. He dismounted, tied the buckskin to the corral post, and then climbed up on the fence to look in.

Moran said it for him, "Black an' white's in there, Kincaid."

Cass spotted the animal too, easily distinguishable from the other dark shapes by the three white stockings and the large patches of white on its flanks.

Stub Moran was silent now, watching him as he took his rope and stepped into the corral. The black and white remained still when he threw the rope on it, and he went over and felt the flank. It was still very warm, damp. The horse had recently been running hard.

Cass recoiled the rope, hung it from the saddle, and walked leisurely toward the bunkhouse. There was a dim light in the windows. A lamp was burning inside the building, but turned down low.

Stub Moran trailed him slowly, keeping a half-dozen paces in the rear. Lifting the latch, Cass went inside. There was a long, rough board table running down the center of the room with a lamp burning at one end. The fireplace was in the center against one wall with the bunks on either side, double tiers, ranging along both walls. There was no fire in the fireplace.

The usual bunkhouse smell greeted him when he opened the door—a mixture of dried perspiration, leather, kerosene from the lamp, the manure smell of men who worked around stables and horses.

About a dozen of the bunks were occupied, and quite a few of the sleepers were snoring stentoriously. Cass hesitated inside the doorway, and then walked down along the table to turn up the lamp. A man cursed from one of the bunks, thinking it was a Slash M rider coming in late.

Stub Moran was standing in the doorway, leaning against one of the sills, watching as Cass moved leisurely past the bunks. Cass couldn't mistake that lank, yellow hair. The young rider's gunbelt hung from a peg above the bunk. He lay with his face toward the wall.

When Cass ripped the blanket from him, he whirled around, lips drawn back in a snarl, coming up in a half-sitting position. Before he could say or do anything, Cass had lifted the gunbelt from the peg and tossed it over on the table. It landed with a bang and other sleepers sat up.

Cass said evenly, "Get down, Cummings."

When the yellow-haired rider didn't respond fast enough, he grabbed his ankle, yanked hard, and threw him heavily to the packed-earth floor. Cummings let out a short yelp as he hit the floor, but he scrambled to his feet like a cat. He looked toward the door where Stub Moran was still standing, saying nothing. Cass moved in between him and the door.

A rider from one of the far bunks called sourly, "What the hell is this?"

They were all awake now, sitting up, some of them sleepy-eyed, but watching. Stub Moran said one word—"Kincaid."

Arch Cummings was fully dressed, except for his boots. He stared at Cass, his greenish eyes glittering in the lamplight. He'd backed up against an empty bunk and he crouched there, lips still drawn back in that snarl, but the fear coming into his eyes now.

Cass said to him, "There's your gun on the table, Arch. You want to use it now while I can see you?"

Cummings didn't say anything. His eyes flicked to the gunbelt on the table, but he made no move to go over for it.

"You shoot better from the brush," Cass told him tauntingly, "or through a man's window when he's sleeping."

Arch Cummings had been watching him

tensely, but his eyes flicked now to the doorway. Cass heard Griff Munson say behind him, "What's this, Kincaid?"

Without turning his head, Cass said, "Reckon you heard it, Munson. Once from the timber along the trace this afternoon, and tonight from the porch roof looking into my room. I spotted his horse running away from the hotel."

He heard Munson coming up behind him, and he noticed that Arch Cummings took a step back along the wall of bunks. Munson said softly, "That right, Cummings?"

Cummings mumbled something about, "I'm through here. I'm gettin' the hell out." His words came close together, and the fear in his face was a living thing.

Cass hadn't expected this. He turned his head to look at Griff Munson as the boss of Slash M went past him. Munson was smiling, but it was a cold, cruel smile, made all the more deadly because he was a handsome man. His eyes were narrowed as he advanced on young Cummings.

Arch Cummings snarled when Munson was about three feet away, "I'm quittin', Munson. You hear me?"

Griff Munson hit him then for the first time. It was a clean, swinging blow with his open hand, a slap full in the face, but with sufficient force to send Cummings reeling along the tier of bunks.

The men in the bunkhouse watched uneasily.

One rider pulled his feet up as Cummings staggered past his bunk, Griff Munson walking after him slowly. He did it all with his open hands, never closing his fists, but it was the worst thing Cass Lorimer had ever witnessed.

It didn't last long—just a few minutes. Munson walked after the cursing, sobbing Cummings. He lashed out with his big hands, driving Cummings' protecting arms away, slapping him across the face with the palms of his hands, with the backs of his hands, cruel swinging blows which were worse than punches because they seared the inside of a man, shaming him.

When Cummings sprawled on the dirt floor, Munson yanked him to his feet again, backed him against one of the bunks, and slashed some more. After a while Arch's face became red and swollen; tears of rage, pain and impotence coursed down his face. He fell on the floor and lay there, sobbing, cursing.

Cass didn't wait to see the finish of it. The sight of the reeling, crying Cummings sickened him, even though he knew that the young Slash M rider deserved it and more. He went outside and walked down to the corral. As he was rolling a cigarette a few minutes later he heard Griff Munson come out of the bunkhouse and walk toward the ranch house. The ranch house screen door closed with a sharp bang.

Cass put the cigarette in his mouth and struck

a match on one of the corral posts. He'd been surprised at Munson's terrific show of temper. Evidently Griff didn't like to be crossed. Cass didn't flatter himself that Munson had lashed out at Cummings because of any liking for his hired gunhand. Munson didn't want Ty Kincaid killed—at least not yet. If Munson suspected that Kincaid was not Kincaid, he had to know who he was; what he was trying to do; and how much he knew before he sent a gun-thrower or a bushwhacker after him.

Chapter Ten

At ten o'clock the next morning Cass waited in the lobby of the Yankee House. He had his buckskin tied at the rail outside, along with a little sorrel mare he'd rented from Farrel, the livery stable man. Farrel had assured him it was the same horse Miss Schuyler had been riding in recent weeks.

Valerie came down in riding clothes, making a very pretty picture. The riding outfit was something Cass had never seen in this country—fawn-colored riding pants, a short jacket with a white blouse, and a narrow-rimmed derby hat. He looked at the hat and said, "Reckon that won't give you much protection from the sun, ma'am."

"I don't believe it was made for that purpose," Valerie laughed. When she saw the sorrel tied up outside she clapped her hands happily. "How did you know I wanted Brown Eyes?" she asked.

Cass grinned a little as he ducked under the tie rack. "Livery stable man called that mare Stew Face," he said.

As he helped Valerie into the saddle he caught a glimpse of Matt Quinn out in front of his office down the street. Quinn had been watching them, but as they turned their horses down the street in his direction, Quinn stepped inside quickly so that they would not see him.

As they moved past the front of his office, the shade was pulled down low, and Cass fancied the lank sheriff sitting in his swivel chair behind that shade, his jaws drooping, a glum expression on his face. He didn't think Matt Quinn would be whistling now.

As they moved up the grade out of town, Valerie said, "John tells me you had a little excitement last night in your room."

Cass nodded. "Maybe a drunk throwing lead around," he murmured.

Valerie looked at him archly. "Would a drunk climb a porch roof to do that?" she asked.

Cass grinned faintly. "Reckon I must have enemies, then," he stated.

"Who?" Valerie asked curiously.

Cass rubbed his jaw. "A man doesn't ask questions like that in this part of the country," he observed.

"Well, after all, I'm not a man," Valerie Schuyler told him glibly. "It seems to me you've made some rather bitter enemies in the short time you've been here, Mr. Kincaid."

Cass shrugged. "Some enemies a man always has," he stated.

It was considerably cooler when they reached the top of the grade, and then turned off the stage road, heading west into the hills.

"Reckon you know this part of the country better than I do, ma'am," Cass said. "You lead the way."

"I've done quite a bit of riding since we came out here in the spring," Valerie told him. "There is some beautiful country up along Wood Creek—beyond the homesteaders' sites."

Cass nodded. "Hearing a lot about Wood Creek," he murmured. "We can have a look at it."

"I was up there on Tuesday morning," Valerie went on, "and I met a very rude old man."

"I'll shoot him," Cass said.

Valerie Schuyler laughed. "I saw him down along the edge of the creek. He had a pan and he seemed to be washing himself. When I came closer to speak to him he told me to go away. He—he even cursed at me!"

"An old man," Cass repeated curiously, "washing himself with a pan?"

"He had a basin full of water," Valerie said. "His face did look rather dirty, though, so I guess he hadn't started to wash when I came up."

A broad grin broke out on Cass's face as the light dawned on him. He said, "Reckon you ran across an old prospector up the creek, Miss Schuyler. They're a crabby lot anyway. Don't like human beings."

Valerie stared at him, bewildered. "What was the basin for?" she wanted to know. "He didn't use it to wash?"

"He was washing sand in the pan," Cass explained. "Those prospectors crawl up every hill and down into every draw looking for color. They spend a lifetime doing it. You'll find their bones from here to the Sierras, and from Canada to the Rio Grande."

"What's color?" Valerie asked curiously.

"Gold," Cass said easily, and then something clicked in his mind. He said it again, more slowly, "Gold." He looked at Valerie Schuyler. "You saw this old prospector up along Wood Creek?"

"Up beyond the last homestead," Valerie told him. "The one which had belonged to—to the McCoys, I'm told."

Cass noticed her hesitancy in speaking about the McCoys. "We could take a ride up there and see your prospector. He might dig up some gold for you."

"I'd like to see it," Valerie laughed.

Cass followed her down into a draw and then up the other side, and he was thinking rapidly now, wondering why the thought had not occurred to him before. Griff Munson was going to great pains to add the Wood Creek homesteads to his range, but not because he particularly needed the water, nor the land. There was something else he was interested in; something, perhaps, which glittered yellow among the sand and stones of the creek, flushed down from the higher slopes to the north and the west.

A crabby old prospector could be crabby because he was a prospector, and he could be so nervous and suspicious because he'd found something—color!

The land here rose in long, gradual steps, and it was a dry land beyond the homesteads. Cass could see the rocky ledges and slopes several miles to the north. The McCoy homestead, or what was left of it, probably lay a little distance to the south of those rocks, along the creek, where the land was more fertile.

Valerie was in good spirits. She let the sorrel run, and she rode very well. Once the little derby hat bounced off her head and Cass had to ride back to scoop it up and dust it off.

They paused to let the horses drink at a little stream which ran into the creek, and when they had climbed back out of the draw again, Valerie said, "The creek is just ahead. It'll be a little hard on the horses getting down to the water, but the sorrel made it the last time I was here."

Cass was anxious to reach this part of the creek now. He didn't think that they'd meet the old prospector because if the man had discovered gold in the creek he'd be hotfooting it to the nearest claims office after staking out his claim along the creek. If he'd found gold in any quantity, Cass would be able to locate his stakes.

They scrambled up the slope, the horses kicking loose shale as they went up, and then Valerie

Schuyler paused on the summit. Wood Creek lay before them now, about a hundred yards below at the bottom of a rocky canyon. A heavy growth of willows grew along the edge of the creek.

Cass looked up and down along the creek. He could see no signs of the old prospector which Valerie had mentioned. The water was not more than a foot or two deep here, studded with rocks because the spell of dry weather had considerably lowered the water in Wood Creek.

"He was right down below," Valerie said.

"You tell anybody about this?" Cass asked her suddenly. "Anybody besides myself?"

Valerie looked at him curiously. "I did mention it to John, but he just laughed and told me not to be too curious the next time. I guess he's forgotten about it."

"No one else?" Cass persisted.

Valerie shook her head. "What is so important about the prospector?" she asked.

Cass frowned. "I'm not sure yet," he admitted, "but if I were you, I wouldn't mention the fact that you'd seen a prospector here grubbing for gold."

"You think he's found gold?" Valerie wanted to know.

"Even the rumor of it," Cass stated, "could bring five thousand men up here. They'd dig up every inch of this creek and the surrounding hills. They'd ruin it."

The explanation seemed to satisfy her. Cass watched her take the sorrel down the slope. It was not as difficult getting down as it looked. The two horses picked their own way down, finding the easiest grades.

They dismounted along the edge of Wood Creek. Valerie had seen the prospector in a spot where the willows were not so thick. Cass watched her walk down to the water to pick up a few smooth, white stones, and then he rolled a cigarette and studied the ground carefully as he did so. The sand was soft here and the signs were very plain even though they were two days old now.

Dismounting, his eyes had immediately spotted the darkened stains on the ground and speckling some rocks at the edge of the water—bloodstains. There were bootprints here, too; two riders had come down to the edge of the water. They'd dragged something back in among the willows. The scuffed path leading back from the creek was very plain.

A shadow on his face, Cass glanced toward the heavy clump of willows off to his right. He was fairly sure what he was going to find now, but he wasn't sure that he wanted Valerie Schuyler to see it. He'd found one dead man on the way in to Red Rock. Another lay in among the willows—two days dead, and he wouldn't be a pretty sight.

Carelessly, Cass edged over toward the

willows. He picked up a stone, tossed it into the water, and then when Valerie looked at the splash he glanced in among the willows. He saw a boot, and then a portion of a man's leg. He walked back to the buckskin and Valerie.

"Reckon your prospector didn't wait for you to get back, Miss Schuyler."

"He *has* run out on me, hasn't he?" Valerie laughed gaily.

Cass was thinking bitterly, *Not of his own will, but he's run out for good, lady!*

He found something else before they climbed back up the side of the canyon wall—a scattered collection of stones. There were about a dozen of them, and they'd once formed a small pyramid. A notched stick with a note in it had once protruded from that pyramid of stones, marking one of the boundaries of the old prospector's claim. The pyramid, the stick and the note had been destroyed by the two killers, but they couldn't erase the fact in Cass Lorimer's mind that the prospector had found color here in Wood Creek, enough color to turn men into killers.

When they reached the top of the canyon the sun was almost straight overhead, and Cass said, "Time to get back if you want your dinner today."

"I enjoyed the ride," Valerie told him, "even though we didn't find our prospector."

Cass didn't say anything to that. They rode along in silence for a while, and then Cass said,

"How long you figure on staying in Red Rock, Miss Schuyler?"

"That depends, of course, upon John," Valerie told him. "He thought he could finish his series of paintings in a year. We've been here nearly five months now."

"Reckon you'll go back to England?" Cass asked.

Valerie shook her head thoughtfully. "We both love it out here," she told him, "and we have no real ties in England. It is possible after John finishes his paintings he will decide to stay somewhere in the West."

Cass had the feeling that Matt Quinn would be very happy to hear this. He felt good about it, himself, because he liked the Schuylers. Both of them.

They were moving past the old McCoy homestead, and Cass saw the fallen-in house, and the sheds, very similar to his brother Jeff's abandoned homestead, weeds growing right up close to the place. Several fruit trees had been set out, and probably watered and tended carefully in the beginning, but they were turning wild now, and they probably would not last long without care.

Valerie Schuyler looked at the place too, but she made no comment, and Cass wondered what she thought about him for taking Katie McCoy out. He'd even had a fight over Miss McCoy. She would undoubtedly have heard about that.

A jack rabbit hopped out of the brush near the shack, and then Cass heard a horse coming up over a slight rise ahead of them. He slowed down when the horse came into view. It was a black horse with a white face, and Katie McCoy was in the saddle.

She spotted them immediately because they were less than twenty-five yards distant. Cass knew that she would have liked to turn away, but it was impossible now. Valerie Schuyler said, "That's Miss McCoy now, isn't it, Mr. Kincaid?"

"Reckon that's right," Cass murmured.

Katie was wearing the same riding costume she'd had on the first afternoon he'd met her—fawn-colored riding pants, a tan shirt. Her copper-colored hair was tucked in under a black, flat-crowned sombrero.

She approached them slowly, nodding as Cass reined in the buckskin. Cass said, "Afternoon, Miss McCoy. You know Miss Schuyler?"

Valerie nodded and smiled. She said, "I've seen Miss McCoy in town. We've never met formally."

"How do you do?" Katie said. Her voice was even, almost cold, and Cass sensed the fact that she was definitely hostile to the English girl. She looked at Cass and then at Valerie.

Cass said to make conversation, "This was your place, wasn't it, Miss McCoy?" He nodded toward the homestead.

"We lived here for a number of years," Katie nodded slowly.

"It's a pity those apple trees are turning wild," Valerie told her. "I love apple blossoms in the spring. Did you ever get any fruit, Miss McCoy?"

"They never came in," Katie told her. She was looking at the trees now, a stony expression on her face. It was very evident that she wanted to go along.

Valerie said, "It was nice meeting you, Miss McCoy. We must have lunch together some day."

"We might arrange it," Katie nodded. She nodded to Cass, and she rode off then.

Cass noticed that she had a Winchester rifle in the saddle holster. He noticed the Winchester because he was becoming very conscious of that particular gun of late. He had an idea that Katie McCoy knew how to use that rifle, too.

Valerie said, as they rode on, "She's a very strange girl, Mr. Kincaid."

Cass nodded. "Reckon she's had a hard time of it."

"And a very beautiful girl, too," Valerie added archly, "or hadn't you noticed it?"

Cass scratched his chin. "Reckon I noticed it," he murmured. He was still wondering why Katie was hostile to him; it was almost as if she were jealous of his riding with Valerie, and yet she'd told him very plainly that she intended to marry Griff Munson. Everyone in Red Rock assumed she was practically married to Griff already.

When they were on the stage road again, heading toward Red Rock, Valerie said reflectively, "Do you think those stories they tell about her can possibly be true, Mr. Kincaid?"

Cass hadn't quite expected that kind of question, and he wasn't ready for it. He said slowly, "Reckon I don't know her well enough, ma'am. You know how those stories circulate once they get started."

He had to admit, though, that Katie had permitted them to get started, and as far as he knew she'd never tried to deny them, and she did live within ten minutes ride of Griff Munson's ranch on the edge of Slash M range. She didn't have to live there; she owned a nice home where everybody thought the McCoys were poor homesteaders, and her father, or stepfather, was reputed to be a shiftless character. She wore fairly expensive clothing, and she had no visible means of support. The evidence in every way was damning; and added to this was the fact that she'd told him plainly she was going to marry Munson some day.

They said no more about Katie the rest of the ride into Red Rock. Cass left Valerie at the Yankee House. She went up to change and he dropped into a lunch room across the road for a bite to eat before riding out again. He was anxious to get back to Wood Creek again. He had to find out definitely why Griff Munson was buying up the homesteads along the creek, forcing the homesteaders out when they wouldn't sell, even hiring professional gunmen to help him. Munson evidently thought there was gold in quantity in Wood Creek, and he was after it—all of it!

Kincaid, the gunman, hadn't known about the gold. The lawyer, Manville, didn't know about the gold. Possibly, aside from Ira Bream, Munson's ramrod, no one else knew. The dead prospector had known, but he wouldn't talk about it now.

The bleak thought came to Cass that possibly his brother Jeff had known, and that was the reason Munson had had him killed. Jeff's wife hadn't known about it, but Jeff had always been a close-mouthed man, and he might have been thinking of verifying his findings before even telling his wife about it.

Stepping up on the walk in front of the lunch room, Cass saw Matt Quinn just emerging from the Double Yoke Saloon, next door to it. Quinn's blue eyes were bleak. He nodded to Cass and said evenly, "Have a nice ride, Kincaid?"

"Getting hot in the hills, too, at this hour," Cass told him.

Quinn looked at him steadily. "For a new man in town," he observed acidly, "you know a hell of a lot of women, Kincaid."

"Only two," Cass smiled, feeling a little sorry for the man.

"Reckon one should be enough for any man," the sheriff of Red Rock scowled.

"You got a law around here like that?" Cass asked softly.

"There ain't," Quinn said morosely, "but there should be."

"I'll buy you a cup of coffee," Cass smiled.

"Had my lunch," Quinn told him. "Buy one for yourself, Kincaid." He walked off glumly, and Cass stepped into the lunch room. He hadn't told Quinn about the dead prospector up on Wood Creek, and he didn't intend to tell him until he'd learned a few more things, himself.

Riding out of Red Rock less than an hour later, he saw Stub Moran coming in. The little Slash M rider pulled up his horse and waited on the edge of the road.

Cass said to him, "What happened to Arch Cummings? He pull out?"

"Out o' Slash M," Moran nodded, "but if I know that crazy kid he ain't leavin' this part o' the country until he gets a few things settled first."

"Me?" Cass smiled faintly.

"You," Moran nodded, "but Griff first. The kid had hell in his eyes when he rode off. He'll never forget that lickin', Mr. Kincaid."

"Didn't figure he would," Cass murmured. He hadn't thought that Arch Cummings would leave the country. The yellow-haired would-be killer had the vindictiveness of an Indian. He'd die now rather than let the terrible beating he'd taken go unrequited. It meant that he, Cass Lorimer, still had to watch the back alleys as he walked, and the hidden rocks and stands of timber as he rode. But there was some consolation in the fact that young Cummings hated Griff Munson now, more than he hated Kincaid.

Moran went on, "Griff gave us orders this mornin', Kincaid. We ain't supposed to know you too well, or cause you any trouble. He gave us that straight. Reckon you're the top hand with this outfit now, along with Ira Bream."

"Griff afraid I'll get hurt?" Cass asked softly.

"Hell," Moran chuckled, "reckon it's the other guy gets hurt when you're around, Mr. Kincaid."

Cass nodded. He looked past Moran down the empty, dusty stretch of lonely road. He was the tough, arrogant Ty Kincaid, and he said thinly, "Passed by the old Lorimer place the other day. Reckon they'd better not try to fix me the way they fixed that Lorimer fellow. Heard about that in town."

He looked at Stub Moran, then. Little Stub's features had frozen. His flattened face drooped. All he said was, "Reckon that's right, Mr. Kincaid."

He'd been there, though, and he knew. Some day he would tell. Cass Lorimer was quite sure about that.

Chapter Eleven

It was past four o'clock in the afternoon when Cass turned the buckskin down into the little canyon through which Wood Creek ran at this point. Moving down from the rim of the canyon it felt as if the heat were coming up to meet him. This morning with Valerie it had been considerably cooler.

Cass gave the buckskin free rein, letting the big animal find its own way down to the bottom. It was very quiet in the canyon. The creek water flowed by soundlessly. At this hour there were no birds in the willows. Looking up, Cass saw an eagle circling farther up the creek.

He dismounted in the little opening where he'd come with Valerie that morning, and then he stepped over to the thick clump of willows and looked in. The body was where he had left it.

Working his way in to one side he had a look at the dead man. He wasn't as old as Valerie Schuyler intimated. His hair was gray and he had a stubble of gray whiskers. Cass figured him to be in his late fifties. He had a thin face and a long, sharp nose. There were two bullet holes in his chest. He lay on his back, arms and legs outstretched, his hat a few feet away.

Cass didn't see his mining pan or pick, or any

other mining equipment. Undoubtedly, these had been sunk in the creek or hidden somewhere so that if the body were eventually found no one would suspect that he'd been washing for gold in the creek. He wondered why the killers hadn't buried the dead man immediately, thus eliminating the possibility of his being discovered and some kind of investigation made.

He came out of the willows undecided as to what his next step would be, and then he glanced up toward the rim of the canyon. He wasn't quite sure what made him look there, but what he saw nearly froze the blood in his veins. Standing in full sight out on the edge of an overhanging rock was Katie McCoy. She was etched against the clear blue of the sky, and it was unmistakably her. Cass recognized the fawn-colored riding pants and the tan blouse she'd worn that morning. He could even see the color of her hair.

Cass Lorimer's jaw sagged. He crouched there, just emerging from the willows, his gun hand inches away from the Colt gun on his hip. He was thinking of the Winchester which had been fired at him from the timber the day before; of someone who'd crouched in the underbrush patiently waiting for him.

"Katie!" Cass whispered. He didn't want to believe this.

He saw the white puff of smoke from the rifle, followed immediately by the sharp report. He felt his body flinching instinctively away from the impact of the bullet.

He wasn't hit, though. The slug passed over his head, and he heard it hit something behind him—something soft and yielding. He heard the choked cry of pain—a man's cry—and then he dropped to the ground, slipping the gun from the holster as he lay.

A gun roared behind him from a point not more than a dozen yards away, down the slight grade which led to the edge of the creek. The bullet grazed his neck as he went down. He could feel it—hot as a coal from a fire, searing the right side of his neck.

He sent his first shot off wildly, not expecting to hit anything, but hoping to disconcert the man behind him. When he came up on one elbow there were two men down there near the water, at the edge of the willows. One man had been hit in the right shoulder by the bullet from Katie's Winchester. He was desperately trying to switch his gun from the right to the left hand.

The second man, a tall, gangling man with reddish hair, in faded blue Levi's and faded blue shirt, had fired that first shot at Cass. A second slug from Katie McCoy's Winchester clipped a twig from the willow branch a few inches from his head. This was enough to spoil his second shot at Cass too.

Cass shot him through the middle, watched him

jackknife as if he'd been struck in the stomach with the butt end of a pole, and then he swiveled the gun on the second man who'd managed to make the switch now. He fired twice at this man before the gunman could get off a bullet with his left hand. He was awkward with that hand, and his shot went wide of the mark.

Both slugs from Cass's gun went home, one through the head, and the other through the chest. The impact knocked the man back down the slope so that he fell into the water. He lay there, his face submerged, the water reddening around him.

The first gunman had fallen face forward and he lay still on the ground, shoulders hunched inward, his head twisted to one side. The gun hand, still holding the heavy Navy Colt, was thrust out to one side, and the gun lay in the full sunshine, the glistening metal reflecting the rays of the sun.

Katie McCoy's Winchester was still cracking from the rim of the canyon wall. It sounded twice, the bullets passing high over Cass's head this time, aimed at the opposite wall of the canyon. The west wall was considerably lower than the east wall down which he'd come, and he caught a glimpse of a horseman racing away with two riderless horses, the horses of the dead men along the creek.

When Cass looked up again at the girl on the

rocks, she was calmly ejecting a spent shell from the rifle. He watched her step back off the rock and disappear from sight. A few moments later she came down the wall of the canyon on the black horse.

Cass was reloading when she came up. He nodded to her, and he said, "Much obliged, ma'am."

"You sound very formal," Katie retorted, "speaking to someone you kissed a short while ago."

Cass grinned. "All right, Katie," he said. He went down to the creek and pulled the dead man out of the water, looked at him briefly, not recognizing him. He didn't recognize the other man either, but both of them could have been Slash M riders. He'd only met or seen half of Munson's crew. When he came back, he said to Katie, "What happened?"

"Saw them from this side of the canyon," Katie explained. "I was riding by. I pulled back from the edge of the canyon and watched them from the rim. They acted rather suspicious. One man held the horses while the other two came down the wall on foot. They waded across the creek very quietly, their guns in their hands. Then I saw your horse down here. I gathered that they were after you."

"Reckon they were," Cass said mildly. "Should have heard them coming across the creek, but I didn't."

"When they crouched at the edge of the willows," Katie McCoy told him, "I came out on the rock with the rifle."

Cass smiled a little. "Looked like you were sending that first shot at me," he murmured.

She looked at him steadily. "Why?" she asked.

Cass shrugged, but he didn't say anything.

There was a cold grin on Katie's face. She said, "You think maybe I was jealous of Miss Schuyler?"

Cass grinned also. "Not you," he laughed shortly.

"What's in those willows that they had to kill you for finding out?" Katie asked.

Cass frowned. He wasn't dealing with a squeamish girl here who would faint at the sight of blood. Katie McCoy had seen two men die, she'd put a bullet into one of the dead men herself. If he didn't tell her what was in the willows she'd go in and find out anyway. He said briefly, "Another dead man."

He had little doubt now that these three men, the two who were dead and the third who was chasing away with the horses, had come back to bury the prospector they'd left in the willows after killing him a day or two before. They'd come back this time with a pick and shovel, and Cass had surprised them coming down the canyon.

If Katie McCoy hadn't been passing at the time, they'd have had a second body to bury with the first. Cass Lorimer thought about that as he started to roll a cigarette and stepped aside to let Katie go by.

She went into the willows, and when she came out Cass had the cigarette going. He looked at her, surprised at the expression on her face. She was gray, stunned. He said quickly, "You know him?"

"My stepfather," Katie McCoy told him slowly. "Who did it?"

Cass was staring at her. "Reckon these hombres knew about it." He nodded toward the men that he'd shot.

"Why would they want to shoot him?" Katie murmured. "He didn't have any enemies in this country, as far as I know. When he sold his homestead to Griff and left for the East I thought he'd never come back."

"Why did he come back?" Cass asked her.

It was beginning to trickle through his own mind why McCoy had come back to Red Rock. Very possibly McCoy had sold his homestead to Munson not knowing why Munson wanted it, and then he'd started to think. Retired on the money Munson had given him, he'd had plenty of time to think. The idea of gold in Wood Creek had dawned upon him, and he'd come back secretly to see if his hunch had been correct. Finding evidences of gold along the upper stretches of the creek above his own homestead, he'd staked out his claim, and then Munson's riders had finished him off.

Katie didn't know about the gold, and he wasn't too anxious to tell her that he knew. She wanted to be Griff Munson's wife, and if Griff got to know that Ty Kincaid knew about the gold there wouldn't be any more waiting. He'd go as fast as poor McCoy had gone.

Katie was looking at him steadily. "You saw my father in the willows this morning when you were here with Miss Schuyler, didn't you? And you came back to have another look."

Cass nodded. "Didn't think she ought to see it."

"Does anyone else know?" she asked.

"Only the hombre who got away with the horses," Cass stated.

Katie McCoy frowned. "I was never very close to my stepfather," she said slowly. "He was shiftless and he didn't make things very easy for mother, but I don't like to see him shot down like this." She looked at Cass again, and she said bluntly, "Do you know why he was shot?"

Cass looked at his cigarette. "He have any money on him?" he asked.

"He'd got some from Griff," Katie told him, "but he wouldn't be carrying all of it with him. I can't understand what he was doing up here along the creek."

"Maybe he figured on taking out another

homestead," Cass offered. "This land up here is still open range, isn't it?"

"It's no land to farm," Katie pointed out. "He'd have known that."

She walked down to the edge of the creek and stared into the water for some time, Cass watching her as he sat on a big rock a few yards away. He wondered if she could see the shining flecks of gold down there in the clear water, or if indeed there were any.

When she came back he could see from her face that she still didn't have the answer. She said quietly, "If you're going back to town, will you send the coroner out here, and I suppose Sheriff Quinn?"

"Glad to," Cass nodded. "I'll ride back to your place with you, if you want me to."

"I'm all right," Katie told him. "Tell the coroner I'll be out here in the morning when he comes with his wagon."

Cass watched her climb into the saddle and start up the canyon wall. Then he threw away his cigarette and walked over to the buckskin. He wondered now if he shouldn't have told her about her stepfather prospecting for gold in the creek, and his opinion that Munson was behind the killing. If he didn't want her to marry Griff Munson that was the sure way to break it up. He told himself that he would remember that and use it when he had to.

• • •

Back in Red Rock he went straight to the coroner's office and gave him the message. The coroner, a rather young man with spectacles, said with some surprise, "Mr. McCoy! Thought he'd left the country long ago."

"He came back," Cass murmured, "to be buried in it."

It was a little after supper time when he found Matt Quinn bellied up to the bar in the Plains Saloon talking with another man. Cass wondered if it was a coincidence that Ira Bream was standing a few feet from Quinn along the bar, drinking with another Slash M rider. Bream saw him come in, and he nodded slightly.

Walking straight up to Quinn, Cass said, "You have a minute, Sheriff?"

Quinn turned around. He was still a trifle cold because Cass had taken Valerie riding, and he said, "What's on your mind, Kincaid?"

"Been a shooting up along Wood Creek," Cass stated.

He saw Bream turn around and look at him. Several other men in the place heard the words and drew closer. Cass told the story very simply, giving only a few of the details. He mentioned that the two loose riders had jumped him when he'd found the body, and that he'd shot them in self-defense. He made it plain that McCoy, though, had been murdered.

"McCoy," Matt Quinn mused. "What's he doin' back in Red Rock?"

Cass shook his head. "Never knew him," he said briefly.

"You see the body this mornin' when you were out ridin'?" Quinn asked him.

Cass nodded. "Reckon I didn't want Valerie to see it," he stated. "I went back later."

"Could have taken me with you," Quinn accused him. "You saw me early this afternoon."

Cass smiled at him. "Could have," he agreed, and he let it go that way.

Ira Bream was puffing on a cigar, listening, his heavy jaws loose, his pale blue eyes narrowed. There was no expression on his wide, fleshy face.

"Why would anybody want to shoot down Labe McCoy?" a man in the crowd asked.

Quinn looked at Cass. "Any idea?" he asked.

Cass shrugged. "You're the sheriff," he observed. "I found McCoy dead—maybe forty-eight hours dead. The coroner will tell you that."

Quinn scowled. "What about these three hombres who jumped you?" he asked. "They have a reason for wantin' you dead?"

Cass poured himself a drink from the bottle the bartender had placed in front of him. He said, "The way I figured it they were coming back to bury McCoy so that he wouldn't be found. I was in their way."

Ira Bream spoke for the first time. He said

softly, "Never was that much fuss about Labe McCoy when he was alive. Why in hell would they want to bury him without anybody knowin'?"

Cass didn't say anything. He downed his drink and he looked at Bream over the rim of the glass as he did so. There was a faint smile in his eyes. He didn't know whether Bream saw it or not.

Matt Quinn was saying grimly, "Three men dead up on Wood Creek; young Bud Horner shot off his horse the other night; and somebody takin' shots at you through your hotel room window. Trouble seems to follow you, Kincaid."

"Reckon I never run away from it," Cass told him. "Those two riders up on Wood Creek I shot in self-defense. Miss McCoy will tell you that."

"You ever see them before?" Quinn asked him.

"No," Cass said. He looked at Bream, then, and he added, "I had a good look at the third one who got away, though."

"What about him?" Quinn wanted to know.

"You'll see him pretty soon, on the coroner's slab—unless he skips the country," Cass said softly.

Matt Quinn was bristling a little. He said testily, "I'm the law in this county, Kincaid. If there's any shootin' to do, I'll do it."

Cass looked at him. He said laconically, "If I'd waited for you this afternoon, Sheriff, they'd be carting me in with McCoy tonight."

That got a general laugh from the crowd. Ira Bream didn't laugh, though. He puffed on his cigar thoughtfully, and after a while he left the saloon.

Cass had his supper alone in the hotel dining room, and he came out on the walk just about dusk to watch the coroner's wagon rattle by, headed south. He stood there, leaning against one of the pillars holding up the awning overhead, listening to the rumble of the wheels, listening until the sound was very faint. He owed something to Katie McCoy. He owed her this much—he couldn't let her marry Griff Munson without knowing the brand of dog Munson was.

Chapter Twelve

After breakfast the next morning Cass strolled around to the coroner's house. He learned from the coroner that McCoy was being buried that afternoon at two.

"Where?" Cass asked him.

"Next to his wife, out at the old McCoy homestead," the coroner informed him. "Labe never figured he'd be buried out here when he left Red Rock a year ago."

"Funny world," Cass murmured.

He was wondering, as he walked away from the house, who would attend the funeral that afternoon. The McCoys hadn't too many friends, and now Katie had been ostracized in Red Rock since she'd taken up the Denton place and associated herself with Griff Munson.

At high noon Cass saddled the buckskin and came out of the livery stable. Riding under the arch he spotted Hilary Manville darting out of his office, coming across the street toward him.

The little lawyer said quickly, "Riding up to Wood Creek, Mr. Kincaid?"

"Reckon so," Cass nodded.

"On—on business?" Manville asked eagerly. "You know Munson is waiting for that land."

"He can wait," Cass said. "I'm attending a

funeral." He saw the disappointment come into the lawyer's gray eyes, and he added, "Your commission can wait, too, Manville."

"I wasn't worried about that," the lawyer said hastily.

"No?" Cass smiled.

He rode away, leaving Manville on the walk, staring after him.

There were about a dozen people at the funeral. The burial ground was on the old McCoy homestead, a small knoll overlooking Wood Creek. A few trees grew on the knoll, and Cass noticed that the ground seemed to be well cared for. He suspected that Katie often came here to her mother's grave.

Morse Claybank and the boy, Louis, were there, and a number of other homesteaders whom Cass did not know. The minister and the coroner had come out from town, and they stood beside the pine-board coffin.

Cass stood a short distance behind Katie. She was alone, a little paler than usual, but composed. When she saw him ride up and dismount, he noticed the faint surprise in her eyes. She nodded to him.

Griff Munson was not there, nor any representatives of Slash M. This was a homesteaders' funeral. Cattlemen usually rejoiced over such affairs.

The service was very brief, probably upon Katie's request. The local preacher read a few words from his Bible, prayed, gave the committal, and the box was lowered into the ground.

Morse Claybank came over to where Cass was standing when the ceremony was over. The nester said slowly, "Can't understand why anybody'd shoot Labe McCoy. Only thing wrong about Labe was his laziness, an' that ain't reason enough to shoot a man."

Young Louis was with his uncle, and he nodded and smiled shyly at Cass.

"How have you been, Louis?" Cass asked the boy.

"Very well," Louis told him.

"Never figured Labe would come back to this part o' the country," the uncle was saying. "Told me when he left he was through. Said he was goin' to settle down in New York or Pennsylvania, where they had some rain once in a while."

Cass said, "Anybody been trying to buy your homestead lately, Mr. Claybank?"

"I know who's after it," the homesteader said grimly, "but he ain't gettin' it." He looked at Cass curiously, and then he added, "Ira Bream stopped at my place yesterday. Wanted to know if you'd offered to buy my place."

Cass smiled. "You tell him I made you an offer?" he asked.

"Said you were here," Claybank nodded. "Didn't know whether you was lookin' for a homestead, yourself, or just talkin'."

Cass watched Katie McCoy talking with the minister. Some of the neighboring homesteaders who'd known her stepfather came over to speak to her, and then they left. The minister and the coroner rode back to Red Rock together, and then Katie was alone. She stood there, looking down at the two graves.

As Morse Claybank was getting ready to ride back to his place, he spoke again to Cass.

"Runnin' an irrigation ditch from the creek back through my corn patch. Only thing will save this country is irrigation. Until the government starts dammin' up the water out this way an' lettin' it out in irrigatin' ditches we farmers will have to scratch an' make out the best we kin. Someday the change will come. I mightn't be alive to see it, but it'll come."

Claybank said good-by to Katie McCoy, and then he drove off with Louis in the dilapidated buckboard. Cass came over and looked down at the two graves, the new one with its fresh earth and a few flowers, and the other one, grass covered and smooth. He said to Katie, "Still have any ideas why your stepfather was shot?"

Katie shook her head. "Sheriff Quinn dropped in this morning to ask a few questions. We're all walking in the dark."

"Maybe not all of us," Cass said quietly.

The girl glanced up at him quickly. She walked away a few paces and sat down on the grass under one of the trees. When Cass came over, she said, "I have a right to know if you suspect anyone."

Cass took off his hat and twirled it around in his hands. He was looking off toward the west, and he said, "I'll make a deal with you, Miss McCoy. You tell me why you're marrying Griff Munson, and I'll tell you who killed, or who had your stepfather killed."

Katie McCoy stared up at him, her lips tight. She sat on the grass, clasping her knees with her hands, and Cass could see that the knuckles were white with the strain as she stiffened. She said slowly, "Is it your business why I intend to marry Mr. Munson?"

Cass Lorimer grimaced. "Making it my business," he said. "I'm trying to help."

"I don't want any help," Katie snapped.

"Reckon it's about time somebody stepped in and helped you," Cass told her, "before you make a damned fool out of yourself."

"Would I be a fool marrying the richest man in this part of the country?" Katie jeered.

"You'd be a fool marrying anybody you didn't love," Cass observed.

"How do you know I don't love him?" Katie demanded.

Cass shrugged. "Do you?"

She got up suddenly from the ground and walked away. Cass watched her pause in front of the two graves and look down at them. Then she swung around, and he could see the tears in her eyes—not tears of mourning for her mother and her stepfather, but tears of hate, terrible hate! She sobbed, "He's going to pay. He has to pay for this. He killed my mother just as much as if he'd taken a knife and stabbed her in the back."

"Munson?" Cass asked slowly.

Katie McCoy nodded. Her shoulders were shaking with emotion; her voice shook, too, when she spoke. "Mother loved this place. It was the only place she'd ever loved after following my stepfather around for sixteen years from one shack to another. We'd been here five years. She planted the fruit trees. She had plans for fixing up the house when we could get a little money. This was the only real home she'd ever had, and then he came along and took it from us."

"Your stepfather sold it to him," Cass reminded her. "It was a legal deal, wasn't it?"

"It was legal, and he paid a supposedly fair price," Katie said bitterly, "but my stepfather didn't want to leave either—not after he'd put in five years on the land and had the title to it from the government. Munson made him sell, or he'd have gotten what Jeff Lorimer got later. He was afraid of that, and he sold out of fear."

"And selling the place broke your mother's heart?" Cass murmured.

"She died when we were getting ready to move," Katie said tersely. "She'd worked herself to death on this place. She knew what was going to happen if they started to drift again—even with the money Munson had paid my stepfather."

"Now you want to marry him," Cass observed.

"I want to marry him," Katie McCoy said, her voice vibrating, "because I want to give him some of the hell he gave to my mother. I want to marry him so that I can pay him back, and I will."

"You'll kill yourself, too," Cass told her.

"I don't care," Katie said recklessly. "He has to pay and pay."

Cass looked down at the ground. "Why should he marry you?" he asked. "He has you fixed up in a place already. Everybody in this part of the country figures you're practically married to him anyway."

Katie laughed bitterly. "They're wrong," she grated. "They're all wrong. Griff Munson never visited me once when Rosa wasn't around every minute. I saw to that. He—he's never even kissed me."

Cass was staring at her. "What about the house?" he asked. "Where did you get the money to fix that up, and how about the clothes you wear?"

"I inherited a little money from my mother's sister who died back east a few weeks after my mother died," Katie told him. "My mother had a little insurance, too, not very much, but it was enough to buy and fix up the Denson place close by Slash M. I wanted to be close to him. I wanted him to see me dressed up, riding around, coming across him occasionally out on the range. It's worked, too."

"What do you mean, it's worked?" Cass asked slowly.

"He's already asked me to marry him," Katie told him deliberately, "and I've accepted."

Cass Lorimer was staring at her. He stepped up and took her by the shoulders, spinning her around so that she faced him. He said grimly, "Maybe you're making a bigger mistake now. He's much tougher than you think. He'll kill you; he'll break your heart before you break his."

"No he won't," Katie laughed coldly.

"He had your stepfather killed," Cass told her. "I can't prove that yet, but I know it."

Katie McCoy moistened her lips. "Why would he have my stepfather killed?" she asked quietly.

"Because," Cass scowled, "there's gold in Wood Creek, and Munson has been trying for a long time to acquire every homestead along the creek. He had Jeff Lorimer killed either because he'd learned about the gold deposits or because he wouldn't sell his homestead. He forced your stepfather off his homestead. He hired me to help him chase out Claybank and the few remaining nesters along the creek. He wants to have every foot of that land for himself when the news of gold gets out."

Katie was staring at him as he spoke. When he paused, she said, "You think my stepfather was prospecting for gold along the creek, and he found color?"

"I know he was prospecting," Cass told her. "Miss Schuyler saw him several days ago. I found the pile of stones he'd set up as claims markers. Munson's riders destroyed the markers and killed your stepfather before he could record his claim. They've been patrolling Wood Creek for a long time. I think your stepfather was curious to find out why Munson wanted the homesteads along the creek. He came back to find out."

Katie nodded. She looked down at the new grave, and then she slowly said, "Who are you? You're not a professional killer, even though you are very fast with a gun."

Cass looked at her steadily. "Who do I look like?" he asked. "Somebody who used to live along the creek, who had a wife and child. He was ten years older than I am."

"Jeff Lorimer," Katie murmured. "You're Jeff Lorimer's brother."

"You're not the only one who owes Munson something," Cass grated.

"How did you get this job with Munson?" she asked curiously.

Cass told her briefly about the dead Kincaid. He said, "I'm stringing along with Munson until I find out who used the gun on Jeff. I don't think it was Munson, himself. He doesn't do the dirty work, but he'll pay to have it done."

Katie McCoy had been watching his face as he spoke. She didn't say anything when he'd finished, and Cass snapped at her. "You still aim to marry him, Katie?"

"Why not?" Katie McCoy asked him tersely. "I have all the more reason now."

Cass Lorimer stared at her. He walked over to the buckskin and climbed into the saddle. Then he turned toward her and said softly, "Another reason why you won't marry Munson, Katie."

"Why?" Katie asked.

"You can't marry a dead man," Cass told her, and he rode away.

He was in a reckless mood as he went back to town. He had the feeling that he'd wasted too much time already, and that very shortly things had to come to a head. While he was positive that Griff Munson was suspicious of him, there had still been no real trouble because Griff had to know more before he played his hand.

Katie McCoy's unreasoning logic in marrying Munson out of hate further complicated matters. There was always the possibility that she would marry him suddenly, secretly, and he didn't want that. Now that he knew Katie had not been living with Griff, or that Griff hadn't paid for her home and her clothing, he had altogether different feelings with respect to the homesteader girl. He couldn't forget, either, that she'd saved his life down there in the canyon.

Riding into Red Rock he saw Valerie Schuyler coming out of a store. She didn't see him as he turned the buckskin into the livery stable alley, and he was thinking as he moved into the cool shade of the alley, *You won't have any more trouble from me, Quinn.*

At six o'clock that evening he noticed Griff Munson's big bay horse tied out in front of the Plains Saloon. Ira Bream's chestnut gelding was next to it, standing three-legged, swishing the flies with its tail.

Coming out of the dining room door of the Yankee House, he saw several other Slash M horses at tie racks along the street. Then Stub Moran came in with three more Slash M hands. Moran waved to him and grinned. Cass nodded back. He smiled faintly, a tough, uncompromising smile. He took a seat in one of the wicker chairs on the porch, and then he slid a cigar from his shirt pocket, biting off the end before putting it into his mouth.

These Slash M hands coming into town tonight meant one thing. Griff Munson had made up his mind. Cass Lorimer felt his pulse begin to beat a trifle faster, but he was glad. The time of waiting was over. Tonight, the boss of Slash M wanted his showdown, and he was going to get it.

Then John Schuyler, the artist, came out through the door from the lobby. He dropped down into an empty chair beside Cass, and he said, "Still hot."

Cass nodded. The heat wave was still unbroken. It was like a thick, oppressive blanket spread over the town. When a horseman went by the dust particles seemed to hang in the still air for long minutes, a dry, powdery cloud. The sounds seemed to be magnified. He could hear a blacksmith pounding a shoe on the other side of town, and the talk from the various saloons along the street seemed excessively loud. In the hotel kitchen off the dining room he could hear the banging of dishes and of pots and pans, and the talk of the help.

John Schuyler said, "Even hot in my place today."

Cass was looking at the horses in front of the tie racks. He said, "Hasn't kept people out of town."

Schuyler laughed. "Saturday night," he explained, and it was the first time Cass Lorimer had been aware of this fact. Most riders came in on a Saturday night when they would stay away during the week. It explained the horses at the tie racks.

Cass felt some of the tension go out of him. He puffed on the cigar thoughtfully and he lifted his boots to the top of the porch rail. Then he saw Stub Moran, who had gone into the Plains Saloon, come out again, wiping his mouth with the back of his sleeve, his hat pushed back on his flat face.

Ira Bream came out of the saloon a few moments later and he stood out on the edge of the walk, his hands in his back pockets. He seemed to be looking straight across the road, but Cass Lorimer was quite sure the Slash M ramrod was watching him up the street out of the corner of his eyes.

John Schuyler said, "Made any progress in your plans here, Mr. Kincaid?"

Cass took the cigar from his mouth. He looked at it thoughtfully, and then he said, "Maybe I'll know more after tonight."

Chapter Thirteen

At eight-thirty that evening Cass stepped into the small Idle Hour Saloon at the other end of town. He'd seen Stub Moran go in there with another Slash M rider a half hour earlier as little Stub made his rounds of the Red Rock saloons.

This Saturday night routine was almost a religious rite with Stub. He had to have his drink, or make his visit in almost every saloon in town.

Watching from the darkened hotel porch, Cass had seen him go from the Double Yoke to the Happy Day. Then from the Emporium to the China Doll. The Idle Hour was seventh on the list for Stub.

The little bar inside the Idle Hour was about half-filled as Cass stepped in. Stub Moran was at the far end, shoulders hunched, holding his head in his hands. For the moment he was alone.

Stepping up beside him, Cass said evenly, "Reckon I owe you a drink, Moran."

Little Stub lifted his head. He wasn't drunk, but he'd had quite a few. His flat face was shiny, and his pale blue eyes bloodshot. Grinning, he said, "Much obliged, Mr. Kincaid."

To the bartender who was coming up, Cass said, "The best. Two glasses."

Little Stub started to swell up a little. He was the nondescript rider now, and a famous gunman was buying him drinks. He said, "Damn glad you're workin' with us, Mr. Kincaid."

Cass poured the two drinks when the bottle came. He said evenly, "I like Munson's crew. I don't have to like Munson."

Stub Moran looked at him. "Yeah," he said, and Cass could see that he agreed with him.

"How long you been eating Munson's grub?" Cass asked him.

"Damn near two years now," Stub scowled. "Too long fer one brand."

"He gets what he wants," Cass murmured. "From the nesters, anyway," he added.

Stub downed his drink. He said, "Heard that you found Labe McCoy up along the creek."

Cass nodded. He wondered how much Moran knew. One of the three men who'd been up in the canyon had ridden back with a story for Griff Munson. Probably some of Munson's riders knew what was going on; the others, like Moran, were just punchers riding his range.

"He wasn't pretty," Cass observed. "About two days dead."

"Hell," Moran laughed, "that ain't nothin' to what Hack Jamison an' Lee Spellman found this mornin' off the stage road ten miles south o' here."

Cass was lifting his glass to his lips. He looked at his reflection in the bar mirror, and he said, "What did they find, Moran?"

"Dead maybe a week, maybe two weeks," Stub Moran told him. "Sittin' there on a log, Hack tells me, like he was waitin' fer somethin'. Shot himself right through the head."

Cass downed his drink and set the glass back on the bar. "You there?" he asked.

"Munson an' Bream went down to have a look," Moran said. "Reckon if I'd seen it I'd be damn sight drunker than I am now. Two weeks dead—at least that much, so Hack says."

"Why would a man shoot himself?" Cass mused, and he was thinking that now Griff Munson knew for sure; he wondered what Munson would do. Griff only knew this—that a stranger was impersonating Ty Kincaid. He didn't know why; he didn't know how much this stranger knew, or who he was. Griff would be jittery about Wood Creek, wondering if he'd found anything out about the gold. With all these questions unanswered, Munson couldn't kill him yet. If he knew about the gold someone else might know, and with a good part of the land along the creek still held by the homesteaders, Munson didn't want to let the cat out of the bag.

In the bar mirror Cass saw Ira Bream coming through the door, his eyes ranging along the bar until they came to rest on Cass. He came over then, leaning on the wood next to Cass, and he said, "You got a few minutes, Kincaid? Griff wants to see you in the back room of the Plains Saloon."

Cass looked at him, wondering if he ought to carry on with the tough, hard front of Kincaid. Deep down in Bream's pale blue eyes he thought he saw some slight amusement. Bream knew.

"I'll stop in," Cass said briefly.

After Bream went out, Cass paid for the drinks, slapped Moran on the back and stepped outside. Red Rock was well crowded now. The dance hall was open farther up the street, and he could hear the noise there. He was thinking of the night he'd invited Katie to the big dance and she'd accepted. That seemed a long time ago, but it was not. He figured back that he'd only been in Red Rock a week or less.

The south-bound stage rattled past him, the six horses kicking up a cloud of dust. He waited for a few moments on this side of the street until some of the dust had subsided, and then he crossed, heading down toward the Plains Saloon.

He saw John Schuyler in a card game with several other men. Matt Quinn was in the place, too, talking with a man at the bar. Quinn looked at him when he came in.

He didn't see Ira Bream, which meant that Bream was waiting for him with Munson. Matt Quinn's eyes followed him as he went down along the bar, stepping through the door to the back room.

The same three men whom Cass had met that first night in Red Rock were in the room. Griff Munson sat at the card table, shuffling the deck. Bream sat in a chair against the wall, the third man leaned against the doorframe.

Munson nodded when Cass came in. "Been wanting to have a talk with you, Kincaid," he said casually.

"Talk doesn't cost anything," Cass told him. He sat down in the chair without even giving the man behind him a second look. He saw Bream push his hat farther back on his head and hook his hands in his gunbelt as he settled himself in the chair.

Munson said, "You doing anything up on Wood Creek, Kincaid?"

"Shot two men who tried to bushwhack me," Cass told him.

Griff Munson smiled at him, but his turquoise-colored eyes were narrowed. "Talking about the homesteaders," he explained patiently, "or have you forgotten about that deal?"

Cass looked at him steadily. "I never forget a deal when there's a dollar in it," he said.

"I'd say," Munson told him deliberately, "that you were forgetting about this one, Kincaid."

Ira Bream said from the wall, "Reckon he's been kind of busy, Griff, sparkin' Miss—" He stopped because Cass had abruptly pushed back his chair and got up.

The man behind Cass moved, too, but Cass didn't look around at him. He got up and walked around the table to stand in front of Bream. Munson watched him without getting up from his chair.

"Finish it," Cass said.

Bream licked his lips. He was a little surprised now, and Cass could see that in his eyes. The Slash M ramrod was a tough man in his own stead, and probably fast enough with a gun. He knew that the man in front of him was not Ty Kincaid, the killer gunman, but he still hesitated, and because he hesitated for even a fraction of a second Cass Lorimer realized that he'd won.

Bream said lamely, "Finish what?"

Cass just smiled at him, then, a slow, taunting, contemptuous smile. He saw the red come into Bream's face, and turned his back on the man and walked back to the table. He didn't sit down this time.

The gunhand in the room had stepped away from the wall, but he was breathing a little faster, a thin-shouldered man with a hooked nose. His green eyes were wide, and his nostrils were dilating.

Cass stood in front of the table, looking down at Munson, and Munson said to him evenly, "You haven't answered my question about Wood Creek, Kincaid."

Cass nodded. He said softly, "Seems like a hell

of a big rush to get these homesteads, Munson. The nesters have had 'em a long time. What's a few more days?"

"When I hire a man for a job," Griff snapped, "I like to have it done. That's all."

"That all?" Cass repeated, and he was smiling now. He took out his tobacco bag and started to roll a cigarette. "Slash M range not big enough for your stock any more, Munson?"

Griff Munson's eyes flicked to Bream. Cass heard the legs of Bream's chair come down on the floor with a light thud. Munson said slowly, "You trying to find out why I'm after that Wood Creek land?"

Cass put the cigarette in his mouth and struck a match. He blew out the first puff of smoke, and then he said coolly, "I don't have to find out, Munson. I know."

There were several long moments of silence. Outside, they could hear the low hum of talk in the saloon, the clink of glasses. Griff Munson looked across at Ira Bream. Bream got up and came behind Munson's chair. He stood there, staring at Cass, the coldness in his blue eyes.

Munson said finally, "All right, mister. We know you're not Kincaid. Who are you?"

"Reckon I could be a government agent," Cass smiled grimly, "checking up on some of these shady land deals out here. Shoot me and find out, Munson."

Ira Bream said sourly, "He ain't no government man, Griff."

Munson didn't think so, either, Cass could see, but neither man could be positive. If he were a government agent and he were shot out here it would bring the whole State Department down on their heads, as well as a lot of publicity which Munson did not want. His plan was to go along quietly, adding one homestead to the other until he had every piece of land along the creek. When the strike came then it would not be on open range country but largely on Slash M property, the deeds for which Munson held.

"Whatever you're trying to do," Munson told him thinly, "you're playing it pretty close to the vest, mister. I could cut you in on this little deal on—on whatever we make out of Wood Creek."

Cass looked at him steadily. "I didn't come here to make deals," he said slowly. "McCoy made a deal with you for his land, Munson. They buried him this afternoon."

"Reckon you're smarter than McCoy," Ira Bream chuckled.

"Nobody's smart," Cass retorted, "with a bullet in his back."

"No deal?" Griff Munson asked.

"Only the kind I make," Cass told him. "I'll let you know when I'm ready to make it, Munson," he added tersely.

He swung around and walked toward the door.

Munson's man still stood there, looking toward Munson for his order to step aside and let Cass out.

Cass didn't wait for the order to come. Grasping the thin-shouldered gunman by both arms he spun him away from the door roughly, opened it, and went out. He hadn't expected them to try to stop him, and they didn't. As he walked down toward the far end of the bar the thought came to him that he didn't have to worry about Asa showing up. He was positive now that Munson had used Asa as a bluff, hoping to find something out about his man.

When he went out on the porch in front of the saloon and stood there for a few moments enjoying the breath of cool air which was sweeping in from the Estrellas, he realized that he didn't have too much time anyway. Griff Munson was playing for very high stakes. A number of men had died already in this game, and more would follow. He had been fortunate thus far that no one had connected him with his brother Jeff, even though he bore some slight resemblance to his older brother. Once Munson connected him with Jeff, the whole Slash M crew would be sent after him like a pack of hounds after a coyote.

Before that time came he had to find Jeff's killer. It might very well be too late after they found out who he was. Stub Moran was still his ace-in-the-hole. Little Stub had the answer.

Moran had left the Idle Hour, and Cass found him in the Paradise Saloon, a little the worse for wear now. When he stepped up to Moran at the bar, another man stepped up on the opposite side of Moran. This man was faintly familiar—a big fellow with black hair, thick-shouldered, dark eyes. He was grinning at Cass, and Cass recognized him as a Slash M hand.

The Slash M rider just looked at him and said nothing, but Cass got the point. Griff Munson wasn't touching him, but Munson wasn't letting him walk around this town unobserved, either. From now on a Slash M rider would always be close by, watching his hotel, watching where he went, who he went with, what he did.

Stub Moran stared first at Cass and then at the Slash M man. He said thickly, "What's up, George?"

"Nothin'," George said. "Nothin' at all, Stub."

Cass flipped a coin in the air and went back to the Yankee House. The town was pretty well filled now with every saloon doing capacity business. Walking past the High Dollar Saloon on the corner of Ramsdell Street, he looked in over the bat-wing doors and he spotted young Arch Cummings drinking alone at the far end of the bar. Cummings had his shoulders huddled over the liquor glass, and Cass got only a brief glimpse of his face. It was a face filled with hate—even now with no one looking at him, drinking alone.

Walking on, Cass wondered how long it would take before Cummings got up enough courage to confront Griff Munson or himself, or if Arch would open up his campaign from ambush again. Arch Cummings being in town further complicated matters. He not only had to watch Munson and his Slash M riders, but he had to be ever careful of the vengeful youth with the yellow hair. Arch had tried to kill him before; he would try again.

On the porch of the Yankee House he stopped and sniffed. The night was still warm despite the little breeze which had come up, but he thought he detected something else in the air, something which had not been there before, something this town had been waiting for for a long time. There seemed to be moisture in the air tonight. It could mean that the long, dry spell was to be broken.

The hotel clerk had a message for him when he came into the lobby. The message was in an envelope and it bore his name.

"Rider from Double Tree brought it in," the clerk told him.

Cass went up the stairs, tearing open the envelope as he walked. The note was from Katie McCoy, and it was very brief. It read:

"They intend to put pressure on Morse Claybank tomorrow. I tried to talk him into coming over to my place, or getting out of sight for a while, but he wouldn't listen to me. I have young Louis with me. Would you talk to Claybank?"

Inside his room, Cass pulled down the shade, lit the lamp, and sat down on the edge of the bed. He looked at the note again and then took the glass globe from the lamp, touched the slip of paper to the flame, and let it burn until the fire almost reached his fingers. Then he dropped the note into the soap dish on the dresser and watched it burn completely.

He knew now beyond any shadow of doubt that Griff Munson had decided to take action. He'd waited long enough, and now he would move, beginning with the homesteader, Claybank. Morse wouldn't sell, but if he were dead it was a different matter. Then, too, his death would frighten the remaining homesteaders along the creek. They'd take what Munson offered them and they'd get out.

For some time Cass sat on the bed in thought, then he got up, turned down the lamp as if he were going to bed, and stepped to the window. Peering out around the shade he could see the corner of Main Street and Grant. There was a dressmaker's shop on the corner, closed and the lights out at this hour. Cass saw a man leaning against the wall there in the shadows under the street awning. He was facing the front of the Yankee House, watching the entrance way. Griff Munson hadn't forgotten him.

Smiling coldly, Cass moved across the darkened room, opened the door and went out into the corridor. He left the door and the window open, the shade still pulled low.

Going down the stairs and crossing the lobby, he noticed that the clerk was asleep behind his desk. The lobby was empty. He went past the desk quietly, sliding the Colt gun out of the holster as he did so. Then, opening the door, he lifted the muzzle of the gun and fired three shots into the air, the slugs just clearing the edge of the porch roof.

Racing back past the startled clerk who'd bounced up from his chair behind the desk, Cass went up the stairs three steps at a time, raced down the corridor to his room, crossed to the window, and looked out. The Slash M man who'd been stationed at the corner was not there anymore. He'd either shifted his position so that he could see into the hotel, or he'd crossed the road to have a look.

Slipping through the window, Cass ran lightly across the porch roof to the far end down which Arch Cummings had gone. He went over the edge, dropping into the rear lot here.

There was the decision to make whether he should swing around to the hotel livery stable and saddle the buckskin, or get another mount for tonight. He decided that Munson would have a man watching the stable, too, and he crossed the vacant lot, came out on the rear street which ran parallel to Main, and hurried up here, turning into Farrel's Livery Stable on Lincoln Street two blocks down.

The livery stable man said to him, "Your buckskin off its hay, Mr. Kincaid?"

"Pulled up a little lame this afternoon," Cass told him. He picked out a dapple gray animal, threw on one of Farrel's saddles, paid in advance for the horse, and rode out.

He kept off Main Street until he was past the last shack along the rear street, and then he swung into the stage road heading south. Again he smelled the rain in the air, very definitely now. The sky seemed to be clouding over. There was no moon, and the stars were disappearing as if rubbed out by a giant hand. This was to be the end of the dry spell, Cass Lorimer knew, and possibly the end of something else too. The end of a long trail which had started in Texas and put him here on this lonely stage road, involving him in a many-sided disturbance.

Chapter Fourteen

Morse Claybank, gun in hand, opened the door when Cass rapped that night, a little after midnight.

"Kincaid," Cass said. "Open up."

The homesteader had recognized his voice. When Cass came in, he said, "You're a late visitor, mister."

He had his pants on, but not his shirt or boots. When he crossed to the bunk to get his boots, Cass said to him,

"I wouldn't figure on any trouble tonight, Claybank. Might as well get your sleep."

The homesteader looked at him steadily after he'd turned up the lamp in the kitchen. His gray hair was standing up on his head. There had been sleep in his faded blue eyes, but he was awake now. He said quietly, "You know about it, Kincaid?"

Cass nodded. "Not Kincaid," he murmured. "Lorimer—Jeff's brother."

Morse Claybank stared at him for a moment. Then he said softly, "No wonder you're standin' up to Munson. Reckon you like him less than I do, mister."

"I had a message from Miss McCoy," Cass explained, "that there'd be trouble here tomorrow."

Claybank nodded. "She took Louis with her. Wanted me to clear out for a spell. I ain't leavin' my land, Lorimer."

"Hold on to it," Cass advised him. "You might be a rich man someday, Claybank."

"Hell," the homesteader smiled faintly, "I ain't figurin' on that, Lorimer."

"What if there were gold in Wood Creek and you own a hundred and fifty acres along it?" Cass asked him softly.

Morse Claybank's eyes started to bulge. "Gold!" he repeated weakly.

"That's what Munson's after," Cass told him. "Labe McCoy found it out and he's dead. I know it, and they'll kill me if they can."

"Gold!" Claybank was saying again, his eyes beginning to glow. "With a little money, Lorimer, we fellers kin do pretty big things around here. We never had a dollar in our pockets to begin with. That's why so many of us get licked. It don't have to be much in that creek—just some, just so's we kin get our feet on the ground."

"As soon as you get the chance," Cass told him, "pass it on to the other homesteaders along the creek. Tell them not to sell. Clear out of the country for a spell if they have to, but *don't* sell."

"Soon as I get a chance," Claybank repeated. "Mister, you don't wait fer a chance to tell about gold!"

He had his boots on, and he grabbed for his shirt as he hurried toward the door. He called back over his shoulder, "There won't be much sleepin' along Wood Creek tonight, Lorimer. You can bet your bottom dollar on that."

Cass heard him out in the rear shed harnessing the old gray. A few minutes later the ancient buckboard rattled up the trace along the creek. Cass put the water kettle over the stove and sat down on the chair in the kitchen. He had the satisfaction of knowing, now, that even if Munson's riders did shoot him down he'd spoiled Griff's plans to control Wood Creek.

He made a cup of coffee, and was sitting at the table, looking over an old newspaper when Claybank came back two hours later.

"John Holbrooke took out his wife's washtub and scooped up a few shovels full of sand from the creek under a lantern light. The sand showed color," Claybank told him.

"Should be better up here, you're closer to the hills," Cass replied.

"I figured that," Claybank nodded. "We had a little meetin' tonight," he went on, "the six of us who homestead along the creek. We decided we'd keep this under our hats till we had staked out our claims and gone to the claims office up in Boswell."

"Good idea," Cass agreed. "You don't want this country swarming with people till you're ready for them." He realized, too, that the delay in spreading the news would give him another day or two to settle his own business in Red Rock. He didn't think Munson would give him much more time than that anyway.

"Most o' the boys will be comin' down here tomorrow," Claybank said, "to stand by me if Munson should send any of his crowd here. We'll give 'em a hot welcome."

Cass didn't say anything, but he was wondering what kind of a hot welcome Morse Claybank had in mind for Munson's professional gunslingers. There might be seven or eight in this nester combine, and probably not one of them could handle a gun.

They had a few hours' sleep that night, Claybank bolting the door from the inside. Cass slept in Louis's bunk up in the loft. Up close to the roof he was the first to hear the rain. It started quietly, gently, with no thunder and no lightning, just an even, steady rain. But in the morning when he got up the rain was still falling and the yard outside was already a morass.

The rain fell out of a gray, overcast sky, and Morse Claybank, looking up at it, shook his head and said, "I've seen it come down fer three days like this. It held up fer a long time, but she's coming now."

"Thought you boys wanted water," Cass reminded him.

"Not so much," Claybank grinned, "that it'll keep us from goin' to Boswell."

Cass went out to look at the gray horse in the lean-to shed. He stood under the shed for a while listening to the rain striking the roof. It seemed to be coming down harder now, as if the main storm were beginning to swing their way.

A buckboard plowed up the trace, and then another. Cass, still standing under the lean-to, saw three men get out of each buckboard. They all carried rifles. These men were the nester friends of Claybank.

Cass watched them unharness the horses in the rain and walk them in under the shed, water streaming from their hats. They came over to shake hands with him, knowing who he was from Claybank's explanation. Most of them had known his brother.

"Sure glad to hear about that gold," John Holbrooke said. "Reckon we owe you a hell of a lot, Lorimer. You want to stake out a claim on my land?"

Cass shook his head. "Anything you find is yours, Holbrooke. You boys have worked hard for what you're getting."

"Gonna be a new life fer us," another one of the nesters said. "My wife's home cryin' about it now. All your life you grub along with your nose in the dirt. Gonna be nice to stand up an' be somebody."

Cass nodded. He was wondering how long they would be able to stand; he was wondering, too, how far Griff Munson would go to keep the creek for himself. Matt Quinn represented law and order in Red Rock, but one bullet in the back would put Quinn aside. After that Munson could be his own law until he'd settled everything to his own satisfaction.

It was cool now with the rain pelting down. Cass watched the nesters troop into the house for a cup of hot coffee. He remained out in the lean-to, himself, wondering if Munson would actually send some of his crew over here, and how far they would go with Claybank.

It was nearly ten o'clock in the morning when they came out of the rain, water streaming down their slickers, dripping from the brims of their hats, the horses' hides steaming. Cass counted six of them pulling up in front of the house. They didn't see him as he stood against the wall just inside the lean-to, keeping in the shadows.

The nesters had watched them ride up, too, and Morse Claybank, a rifle under his arm, came out cautiously, unmindful of the rain which was soaking him to the skin. He wore a hat, but no other protection from the rain, and he stood there in front of his door, looking coldly at the Slash M riders.

None of the Slash M men dismounted. Two of them Cass recognized as men he'd seen out at the ranch house, but the others he didn't know. He'd half-expected Ira Bream to be with the crowd, but Bream was not there. The leader evidently was a thin-faced little gunman with a very wide mouth and a hawk nose. Cass had never seen this man before.

The little man, riding a blue roan, pushed up to the front. Cass could see that his slicker was unbuttoned and his gun free. He said to the farmer, "You Claybank?"

"Reckon that's right," Claybank said and he spat in the mud. "There's six men inside the house with rifles, watchin' you boys every minute. Thought you'd like to know."

The thin-faced man grinned. He shook water from his hat and glanced back to the men with him. He said, "This is a friendly visit, Claybank. What in hell are the rifles for?"

"Insurance," Claybank told him tersely. "You got anything to say, mister, say it, an' then git off my land."

The six Slash M men sat there with the rain pelting them. They sat motionless on their mounts, and then the thin-faced man said softly,

"You ain't too friendly, are you, Claybank?"

"Don't aim to be friendly," the farmer told him. "Slash M ain't never been friendly to me, nor to any o' the boys along this creek."

Cass shifted his position a little in the shed so that he could command the entire six men out in front of the house. Fortunately, the lean-to had been erected some distance to the side of the house, about twenty yards to the rear, and he could see everything that was going on from his position. The pouring rain helped to conceal him from the riders in the front yard.

"Munson," the thin gunman was saying, "won't be pleased when he hears about this, Claybank. We want to be good neighbors, an' you chase us off."

"I'm askin' you to git off my property," Claybank told him grimly.

"We're gittin'," the thin man grinned. He swung his horse around, nodding to the five men with him, and they headed away from the house.

Surprised, Cass lost sight of them for a moment, but not for long. He heard the sudden drive of their horses' hoofs, and then they came into sight behind the house; splashing through the mud directly in front of the lean-to. There were no windows at the rear of the house, making it impossible for the homesteaders inside to shoot at them.

Intent on getting up close to the wall of the house, the six Slash M men still didn't see Cass inside the lean-to, even though some of them weren't more than five yards from him when they dismounted.

Gun in hand now, Cass remained in the

shadows, waiting. He saw Morse Claybank running from the front of the house, shouting for the men inside to come out. Evidently Claybank knew what they could and would do protected by that rear wall. If they could set fire to it some way they could pick the homesteaders off as they ran from the burning building.

Two of the Slash M riders stepped away from the rear wall of the house as Claybank ran back toward them. Cass lifted his gun, leveled it, and fired one shot into the wall a few inches above the head of the nearest man.

He stepped away from the wall as he fired, coming out to the edge of the lean-to, and he stood there, the gun steady in his hand. The six men by the rear wall swung around on him, but only one threw a shot. It was the thin-faced little gunman. The rain pelting down on him, he fired from his slicker, his bullet gouging into the wood of the lean-to upright holding up the right side of the shed.

Cass sent one shot at him, and the little Slash M rider cringed and staggered back against the wall of the building, his gun dropping from his hand into the mud. He went down on his knees in the mud and then he put both hands into the mud and he swayed there, his hat falling from his head just before he collapsed.

Morse Claybank was at the corner of the building with his rifle, and the other homesteaders were running down, also, coming recklessly through the rain.

It was Cass's gun to the rear of them which stumped the five remaining Slash M riders. They didn't like the sight of him standing there at the edge of the lean-to, ready to fire again. If they opened up now they would be caught between a murderous cross-fire. The homesteaders had come down both sides of the building, and they were spreading out a little, their rifles held in readiness, grim-faced men who were fighting for their homes.

Cass waited coolly, giving them plenty of time to make up their minds. One of the men called sharply, "That you, Kincaid?"

Cass didn't say anything. The fighting was over—at least this part of it. Morse Claybank came up closer, still gripping his rifle tightly. He looked at the man lying in the mud, and he said to Cass, "There's one of 'em won't bother us, Lorimer."

The five Slash M men looked at Cass curiously, and one of them said, "Thought you was Kincaid. You change your name, mister?"

"Ask Munson," Cass told him. As he watched the five men mount, he realized that now the cat was out of the bag. Within an hour Griff Munson would know that he was a relative of the dead Jeff Lorimer, which meant that he was not a government man and, therefore, fair game. The entire Slash M crew would be sent out to bring him down.

They'd picked the dead man out of the mud and tied him across his saddle. They rode off that way in the rain, and only the dead man's hat remained, upturned to the rain, the water beginning to fill it.

Buttoning his slicker, Cass stepped out from under the lean-to, picked up the hat, and came back to hang it on a peg inside.

The homesteaders came in under the shed, also, and Morse Claybank said tersely, "Reckon that's the start of it, boys. Munson ain't finished with us, though."

"If it's gonna be a fight," one of the men scowled, "I vote we git Sheriff Quinn out here. We own these homesteads legally, an' Munson ain't got no right to chase us off."

Morse Claybank looked at Cass as if for advice. He said slowly, "Sheriff McElroy was Munson's man at the time your brother was shot, Lorimer. We don't know about Quinn. What do you think?"

Cass shrugged. "Reckon Quinn's all right," he said. "He should be told."

They watched him as he threw the saddle on the dapple gray, and then Claybank said, "We're obliged for your help, Lorimer. Reckon they'd have run us out if you hadn't been in this lean-to."

Cass nodded. "My fight, too," he observed.

He noticed as he stepped into the saddle that the rain seemed to be coming down harder than before, and that a wind was beginning to drive it. The early morning rain was becoming a storm. He figured that by nightfall it would be blowing with gale force.

Claybank called after him as he rode away, "If you pass by Miss McCoy's, Lorimer, you could stop in an' tell her we're all right. Louis is worryin'."

Cass nodded and lifted a hand. He rode off with the rain beating at his back, and he was thankful for the protection of the slicker. The trace up from the stage road was a mass of mud and he had to ride off on the shoulders where the ground was a little firmer.

As Cass rode back to Red Rock he wondered how soon Munson would come after him. He didn't imagine that Griff would be wasting much time. Knowing that he was Lorimer, Munson would also know why he'd come here.

It was high noon when he reached the Denson place, the rain still driving at him, and the wind beginning to blow harder if anything. Despite the hour they had the lamps burning inside the house.

Dismounting behind the house, Cass led the gray into the barn there, and then walked around to the front. Katie McCoy had seen him from the window, and she opened the door.

Cass saw Louis Claybank in the room behind

her, and the Indian woman making the dinner in the kitchen. Katie said quietly, "Come in. It's an awful day to be out riding."

Cass slapped the water from his hat before stepping into the room, and he shucked off the slicker, hanging it on a peg outside the door. He said briefly, "I got your note and I went out to Claybank's last night."

He nodded to Louis and gave him a smile. The boy hung back a little, but worry was in his dark eyes.

"We're ready to have our lunch," Katie said. "I'll have Rosa set another plate." She looked at Cass intently, and she said, "Have any trouble?"

"Some," Cass murmured. "Six Slash M riders came out to see Claybank."

Katie bit her lips, and some of the color left her face. She didn't want to look at Louis now. She said slowly, "What happened?"

"Five of them rode away," Cass stated. "Morse said to tell the boy and yourself that everything is all right."

Relief came into Katie McCoy's deep blue eyes. "I'm glad," she smiled. Then her face clouded. "They'll come again, won't they?"

Cass nodded. "Claybank has a half dozen other homesteaders with him. He's sending word in to Sheriff Quinn that they're expecting trouble. Then there are other farmers up that way who might join in with them."

"There won't be any fighting in this weather," Katie said. "That's one consolation anyway."

"Not between Slash M and the homesteaders," Cass murmured. "Reckon that fight's postponed."

Katie sat down on the edge of a chair. She said quietly, "What are you talking about?"

"Munson knows who I am," Cass told her. "That's one fight the weather can't stop."

Katie McCoy was staring at him. She said slowly, "You mean Griff will send his whole Slash M crew after you?"

Cass nodded. "After they're dead he might come himself." He added thoughtfully, "He might even come first because he's playing for big stakes now."

Katie turned to the boy who was sitting near the fireplace, listening, looking into the flames. Katie had a fire going this morning because it had turned cold with the rain. She said to Louis, "Mr. Kincaid, here, is really Mr. Lorimer. Jeff's brother." To Cass she said, "Louis knew your brother's family well. I believe he used to go over there frequently."

Louis looked at Cass with his dark eyes. "I used to milk the cow when Mr. Lorimer was away. Mrs. Lorimer never could do it right."

Cass smiled at him. Then he said seriously, "I don't suppose you were anywhere around, Louis, when my brother was shot?"

The boy nodded unexpectedly. Katie had been

getting up to go in the kitchen, but she stopped now and stared at Louis Claybank, and then at Cass.

Cass said evenly, "Did you see the shooting, Louis?"

Again Louis nodded. He was pale now, and fear was in his eyes. He said, "I—I never told anybody. I knew if I told Uncle Morse about it they might come and kill him the way they killed Mr. Lorimer. I couldn't tell Sheriff McElroy because he knew about it. I saw him talking with the Slash M men up along the creek before they came down to Mr. Lorimer's place."

Cass got up and stood before the fire. "Tell us the whole thing, Louis," he urged.

Louis Claybank took a deep breath. "Uncle Morse had gone into town that night," he began. "I was alone at the house. I remembered that Mrs. Lorimer had asked me that morning to bring her a few pounds of sugar until she was able to get to town. I thought I'd take it out that night right after supper. I could walk up to the Lorimer place in fifteen minutes."

"You were walking along the creek when you saw Sheriff McElroy and the Slash M riders?" Cass asked.

"I heard them first," Louis explained, "and I hid in the willows along the creek. There was a bright moon and I could see them easily. I knew

Sheriff McElroy, and I knew some of the other riders. Mr. Bream was with them."

"Bream," Cass murmured.

"Sheriff McElroy seemed to be going toward town," Louis went on, "and Bream and the others went toward the Lorimer place. I followed them on foot, keeping well behind."

"You saw the shooting, then," Cass said.

"I was out near the barn," Louis told him, "when Mr. Lorimer came out of the house. I think he'd been drying the dishes right after supper. He had a towel in his hands. When he was shot he fell back on the step in front of the house, and he pressed the towel against the wound in his chest. Then he fell over."

"Who fired the shot?" Cass Lorimer asked softly.

"Mr. Bream," the boy said. "There was only one shot fired. Mr. Lorimer didn't have a gun with him."

Cass put both hands on the mantelpiece above the fireplace, and he looked down into the flames. "Much obliged, Louis," he said quietly.

He heard Katie McCoy say behind him, "Dinner is ready, Mr. Lorimer."

Cass turned around to look at her. He said softly, "Not for me, ma'am."

She didn't say anything for a moment, and then she said, "You'll need a cup of coffee anyway."

Cass nodded. He watched her walk into the

kitchen, and then he placed a hand on Louis Claybank's shoulder, squeezed it a little, and followed Katie. She was pouring the coffee when he came in. The Indian woman had gone out into the rear shed.

Katie said flatly, "You're a fool if you go down there, Mr. Lorimer. That's what Munson wants."

Cass smiled a little. "That's what he's not expecting," he corrected her. "Reckon he's looking for me to hide somewhere. He might have his crew now heading up toward Claybank's place."

Katie sat down at the table across from him. She said, "Why not bring Sheriff Quinn in on this? We have a witness who saw Bream shoot your brother. Louis is old enough, and his testimony will stand in a court."

Cass sipped the coffee. He said briefly, "Munson doesn't like witnesses. You buried your stepfather yesterday. He was a witness to something. I believe my brother Jeff was a witness of some kind. I was a witness up along Wood Creek when you saved me with that shot from your Winchester."

"Louis is only a boy," Katie murmured.

"He's a boy," Cass told her, "but he was smart enough to know that if he opened his mouth about that murder he would be killed, and his uncle. How would you like to bury Louis the way you buried your stepfather?"

Katie didn't say anything. She watched him drink the coffee and put the cup down. Then she said, "You can't fight a whole outfit, alone."

Cass smiled. "Reckon I won't be fighting them all at once," he said. "Bream is the man I'm after—and the man who sent Bream." He looked at her steadily, and he said, "You still aim to marry him?"

Katie looked at the table. "No," she said slowly. "It wouldn't work."

Cass got up. "What about his sister? I met her one day over there."

"Nina's a lovely girl," Katie said promptly. "Griff told me he planned to send her back East. She has an aunt there. He thought it was too lonely for her at the ranch house."

Cass scowled. "I don't like to kill him because of Nina," he said.

"You don't have to kill anybody," Katie snapped. "There's the law."

"The law didn't work," Cass reminded her, "for you and your mother."

"I'm willing to forget that now," Katie said quietly.

Cass looked at her. "A man can't forget," he stated. "Not like that."

She stood in the doorway as he put on the slicker under the low porch roof. Cass said, "Obliged for the coffee. I'll stop in for another one someday."

"I'll wait for you," Katie told him.

Cass looked at her. He could have said more, much more, but under the circumstances there wasn't too much that could be said. He knew how small the prospects were that he'd get through Slash M to Bream and Munson, and still come out of it alive. But it was something—like the pot of gold at the end of the rainbow.

Riding south away from the Denson place, moving in the direction of Slash M, Cass Lorimer knew very definitely that Katie McCoy was the girl for him. Matt Quinn could have Valerie Schuyler, but it had always been Katie from the first time he'd seen her at his brother's abandoned homestead.

Sheets of cold rain swept at him as he moved up a grade and came into the Slash M trace, or what there was of it which was not under water. The slicker buttoned tight around his neck, his hat pulled low over his face, Cass followed the trace, wondering if there would be any other riders out in weather like this. There was the good possibility that even Slash M would wait until the storm abated before looking for him. He couldn't wait, himself, not after waiting this long. There was a driving force inside of him which would not let him go. He knew that he would have no rest until he'd paid off the debt.

Cass was within two miles of the ranch house, still following the trace when he came upon fresh tracks in the mud. Tracks didn't last too long with the rain pelting down into them, but these were very fresh, possibly made a matter of minutes before. On a clear day Cass was sure he would have been able to see the horsemen who'd left the trace to head north in the direction of Wood Creek. In this blinding rain the visibility was limited to less than a few hundred yards.

He counted more than a dozen horsemen in this group, and he knew who they were and where they were going. This was Munson's crew heading back toward Claybank's homestead, gunning for the man who's already shot down three of them.

Thinking of the half dozen homesteaders at Claybank's, Cass frowned. Morse Claybank had stood up to Slash M and it might go hard with him now. In this weather they wouldn't have had time to get reinforcements, and Sheriff Quinn would not be out to Wood Creek.

Hesitating for one moment, Cass left the trace and rode after the fresh hoofprints in the mud. Knowing the general direction they would take to Claybank's he was able to leave their trail after a while, swing around to the north at a sharp trot, and come across in front of them. They would not be moving at a very fast pace in this kind of weather, and he had little difficulty intercepting them when they were still several miles south of Claybank's.

He crossed back and forth several times, seeing no tracks in the mud, and then he spotted them looming up out of the sheets of rain about two hundred yards away. They saw him at the same time, and he saw the lead riders pull up.

Sitting there astride the gray horse, he watched them for several moments, thankful now that he'd taken time to select a good animal at Farrel's livery. He wished, though, that he had the buckskin between his legs; he had no doubts, then, that he could lose these Slash M riders.

They were coming on again, not quite sure who he was, unable to see him too clearly in the rain. Cass waited until they were within a hundred yards, and then he sent the gray horse flying north away from Claybank's.

He heard a man yell, "That's him!"

A shot followed, then another, but it was poor shooting in this weather and he was already dipping down into a hollow when the first shot came. He swung west again, trying to keep a small ridge between himself and his pursuers. He could hear them coming on now, and he hoped fervently that the gray horse wouldn't slip in the mud.

Scrambling up out of the hollow, he opened up a wider gap between himself and his pursuers. More bullets came after him, but they were wild shots. He had them on his tail now and he intended to keep them there, taking them far to the north and west, across Wood Creek if possible, and into the rocky, barren country on the other side, a good place in which to lose himself.

The dapple gray ran as if it loved to run, and it was as sure-footed as a goat even on this sloshy ground. He passed within a mile of Katie McCoy's place on his trek north with the Slash M riders still several hundred yards behind him. He'd already discovered that they had no horses capable of catching up with him, but they were sticking to his trail, hoping that they would eventually run him down.

He went through a stand of timber a half mile north of the Denson place, hammered down a corduroy road which at one time had served lumber men up here, and emerged on the other side. Instead of cutting straight across open country again, leaving plain tracks for them to follow, he cut directly west through the timber, the gray galloping through the trees on a bed of pine needles, leaving very faint tracks.

He'd lost sight of the Slash M men, and he knew it would take a little time for them to find out where he'd left the corduroy road. In a group of a dozen or fifteen men there would be at least one who knew how to follow a horse track even in rain like this, and over pine needles, but it would take time. He was positive he could gain a full half mile on his pursuers which would put him out of their sight. On the other side of Wood

Creek, in order to throw them off his track, he would need a little breathing space.

Fifteen minutes after he left the corduroy road, he dismounted to breathe the horse. He couldn't hear any sounds of pursuit now, but he was positive they would be coming.

When he came out of the timber, five miles west of the corduroy road, he was within a mile or so of Wood Creek. He went down the slope into the creek, which already was beginning to swell, and emerged on the other side.

The gray horse was beginning to feel the pace now because of the slippery footing. Once the big horse nearly went down in the mud. Again, Cass dismounted to give the animal a rest, and then he thought he heard other horsemen coming up in the distance.

The rain seemed to have abated a little. It was no longer coming down in blinding sheets, but it was raining steadily. The water flowed steadily from the rim of his hat. It dripped from his chin and it got inside the collar of his slicker. The slicker didn't fully cover the lower portions of his body, and his pants legs were wet over the boots. Water had seeped into the boots, too, making his feet wet.

It was time to think now of eluding his pursuers altogether and, as he rode south again along the creek, he looked for a rocky ledge down which he could ride into the water.

He found this ledge a mile or so below the spot where he'd crossed, and he worked the gray down the slippery slope until he was in the water at the edge of the creek. He'd left no hoofprints showing that he'd even gone into the creek.

Moving down the creek in the shallow water along the shore, he crossed about a half mile down, coming out again on rocky ground on the east bank. Then once again he went into a tract of timber, riding on pine needles. When he came out of the timber he found his bearings and headed straight for Slash M.

Chapter Fifteen

Moving down into the meadow in front of Slash M, Cass saw the lights already on in the ranch house. The meadow was sloshy from the day-long rain, and the hard-packed ground around the corrals and the bunkhouse had been turned into a morass.

Riding up slowly, Cass dismounted at the rear of one of the barns. The falling rain and the dusk made it an easy task to slip up to the bunkhouse and look through the rain-streaked window. He wasn't sure whom he would find here, if anyone. Bream, undoubtedly, had headed that crew which had gone out after him, and possibly Munson was with them too.

Two men were in the bunkhouse playing seven-up. He didn't know either of them. The long ride and the cold had made him hungry. He was beginning to shiver a little as he stood outside the window, and the thought came to him that a cup of hot coffee and a steak would go good now.

The cook's shack adjoined the bunkhouse, but there was a doorway and a corridor separating the two buildings. Swinging past the door of the bunkhouse, Cass stepped up to the cook's shack and walked boldly in.

He was gambling now on the prospect that the cook did not know any of these men too well. Munson had undoubtedly been hiring new riders all the time, and many of them were out at line camps. The cook's job was to feed mouths, and he didn't care whose mouths they were. He'd seen Cass the first afternoon Cass had come out to the ranch, but he wouldn't know his name, and he probably wouldn't know or care who Munson's riders were chasing back in the hills.

The fat-faced cook turned around when Cass closed the door behind him and sat down at the little side table off the kitchen. He glared at Cass and said sourly, "What in hell do you want, mister?"

He was a big man, big in the shoulders, big in the stomach, thick arms. Cass said to him easily, "The boys will be riding in about an hour from now. Bream sent me on ahead."

"An hour," the cook snarled. "I got the damned supper ready to eat. Who's gonna eat it?"

"Reckon I'll have mine now," Cass told him easily. "I have to go in to town."

"You'll have yours now?" the cook repeated grimly.

Cass took off his hat and slapped it on his knee. He said softly, "You heard what I said, mister. Now."

The fat cook grumbled some more. He let out a long stream of oaths as he slapped a big steak into a plate, scooped out a shovelful of French fried potatoes, and slid the plate onto the table. He slapped two biscuits down beside the plate, and then he poured a steaming cup of coffee from the huge pot on the stove.

"Obliged," Cass smiled. He started to cut the steak. "Munson around?" he asked.

"Ask him," the cook snapped.

Cass's smile broadened. He rather liked this—eating Slash M grub while Slash M was out chasing him in the rainy hills. He wondered how long Bream would keep on the trail before giving it up and riding back to the ranch house.

When he finished one cup of coffee he slid the cup across the table for another, and he started to feel better. He was finishing the steak when little Stub Moran walked in from the rain, water dripping from his hat, his clothes soggy. He started to say to the cook, "Hell's Bells, this weather—"

Then he stopped and stared at Cass at the table. Cass had slipped his Colt from the holster and was leveling it at the little man, the barrel resting on the edge of the table. He held the gun with his left hand as he continued to eat with the right. He said to Moran, "Sit down, Stub."

Moran gulped. He said weakly, "They—they're chasin' you, ain't they?"

"Reckon they are," Cass nodded. "Where's Munson?"

"Rode in to town early afternoon," Moran said. He looked at the gun in Cass's hand, and he swallowed again. "You ain't Kincaid," he said.

"No," Cass told him. "Bream out with the crew looking for me?"

"Yeah," Moran nodded. "You're Lorimer, they tell me. That nester's brother." He started to grin and he said, "You got a nerve comin' in here, mister, an' eatin' Slash M grub."

The fat-faced cook was looking at Cass suspiciously now, but he wasn't armed. He said to Stub, "Who's this hombre, Stub?"

"Kincaid feller," Stub told him. "Man they're chasin' out in the hills."

"He ain't in the hills now," the cook scowled.

Stub was grinning as he sat down opposite Cass. "Maybe you ain't Kincaid, mister, but from what I hear you ain't far behind him. Heard you shot up Sam Fisher out Claybank's place."

Cass shrugged and he went on eating with his one hand.

"An' them two hombres from Galeyville up on Wood Creek when they went up there to bury old man McCoy," Stub said softly. He scratched his chin and said, "You ain't so bad with that hogleg, Lorimer. What do you figure on doing next?"

"Killing Ira Bream," Cass said simply. "He shot my brother, didn't he?"

Stub Moran didn't say anything, but it was in his eyes. He'd been there. Cass finished his second cup of coffee and he pushed his chair back. He said to Moran, "Still raining, Stub?"

"Be rainin' for a week," Moran told him. "You goin' in to town, Lorimer?"

Cass nodded. "Tell Bream I'll be waiting for him there," he said.

The admiration was in Moran's eyes again. He said softly, "Hell, you're fightin' the whole outfit, Lorimer."

Cass put on the slicker he'd taken off and draped across a stool in the kitchen. Moran and the cook watched him silently. They looked at him as if he were already dead.

Moran almost shouted, "You can't fight a whole outfit, Lorimer!"

"Reckon I can try," Cass smiled at him. He nodded his thanks to the cook for the meal and he stepped out into the rain again. He noticed that the wind was beginning to blow, throwing the rain at him in blinding sheets.

The dapple gray was huddled against the wall of the building with the overhang of the barn roof protecting it from the rain. Cass stepped into the saddle and rode away. Riding past the corrals he glanced back and he saw the kitchen door open, and Stub Moran standing just inside it, looking out into the night. He had an idea that Moran would be riding to town tonight to see the fireworks.

The dapple gray sloshed through the mud of the

road, finding its way home almost by instinct. The rain swirled around them, seeming to come from all directions. Cass bent his head and gave the gray free rein. He slowed up when they reached the top of the grade and he could see the lights of Red Rock twinkling below. Griff Munson was down there, and very shortly Bream and the Slash M riders would be coming in. There was the good possibility that they were already here, having given up the chase for him and come into town, thinking he would head that way.

Instead of riding down Main Street he swung off the stage road and came in again around the back street, turning into Lincoln and the Ace High Livery.

Farrel, the livery stable man, stared at him as he walked the gray in through the opening. He scratched his head and he said, "You been ridin', mister?"

"That horse needs a rubdown and a warm blanket," Cass told him. He stood there inside the entrance way, water streaming from his slicker. "Sheriff Quinn in town?" he asked.

"Wouldn't know," the livery stable man shook his head.

Cass frowned a little. On a night like this no one would be moving out of doors. If he wanted to learn anything, he'd have to find out for himself. Then he saw Ira Bream's chestnut gelding in one of the stalls down the line. There were other horses here, too, horses which had been ridden hard that day, bearing the Slash M brand on the hip. They were still wet and steaming a little.

Rolling a cigarette with his wet fingers, Cass said idly, "When did Bream get in here?"

"Half hour ago," Farrel told him. "Mad as hell. He's a tough one, that Bream."

"Is he?" Cass murmured.

As he lighted the cigarette he was thinking that it was a queer quirk of fate that Bream had decided to stable his horse tonight in the Ace High Livery when there were a half dozen other liveries in town. If he hadn't stopped to eat at Slash M he would have walked right into Bream and some of the Slash M crew which had come in here.

Farrel said, "Change of clothes would do you good, mister."

Cass nodded absently. He wasn't going to get that change of clothes just yet. Slash M riders would be watching the hotel again, waiting for him to turn up if he had the nerve. They would be watching every part of this town tonight, ready to shoot him down on sight, and he could expect help from no one. He couldn't go to the sheriff of Red Rock with the statement he'd come here tonight to kill a man, and that he wanted protection while he was doing so. He had to fight Slash M alone—and separately—if he wanted to live.

His slicker collar buttoned up again, he walked out into the rain. He kept one button opened halfway down the raincoat so that he could slide his hand in easily for the gun if he had to.

Crossing Main Street at a quiet intersection, he walked quickly up another street and came out behind the Yankee House. With the rain squalls tearing at his slicker, he came down along the side of the building to the porch. He could hear the rain pounding on the roof overhead.

It was impossible to see very far in this weather. He could not be sure that a Slash M man was not in one of the darkened doorways opposite the hotel on Main Street, another in the lobby, and a third seated in his darkened room, a Colt gun in his lap, waiting for him.

From his position here, Cass could see that Main Street was deserted. There were no horses at the tie racks. Yellow lamplight streamed from saloon windows, illuminating the sea of mud which was the road.

Diagonally across from the Yankee House a door opened and a man came out, head bent against the wind and the rain. Cass saw him cross and duck under the wooden awning opposite the hotel.

The passage of the stranger gave Cass an idea. He had to locate Bream and Munson somewhere along the street. The easiest way to do it was to walk down Main Street, looking through the various saloon windows. With the slicker buttoned up and his hat pulled low across his face he would be difficult to recognize unless they got a good look at his face.

Fading back further into the darkness along the wall of the hotel, Cass suddenly darted across the road into a vacant lot, made his way down a narrow alley, and came out on Main Street a few doors up from the Yankee House. There was an overhead awning here and he was protected from the rain.

The sound of the rain pounding on the wooden boards overhead was deafening. Water rolled from the roof in steady streams; it trickled down through cracks and holes in the roof.

It was dark here. There were several residential houses and a few stores on this block, interspersed with saloons. Stepping to one of the doors, Cass opened it and closed it sharply, the door banging. He started to walk down the boardwalk, his boots making a lot of noise on the wood.

Crossing the road, stepping carefully through the mud, he came up under the awning directly opposite the hotel. There was a man standing in the darkened doorway there. He could see the cigarette glowing in the darkness.

Head down, Cass moved past him, nearly bumping into a man who was coming the other way. He swung around this man and continued down the street, passing the Yankee Bar, the Idle

Hour, passing Hilary Manville's closed office.

He managed to look in over the bat-wing doors of both saloons as he went by, and he noticed that there were only a few patrons in each one. He remembered, then, that this was a Sunday night and, while the saloons were open after six o'clock, not too many riders would come out in this weather, and even the townspeople would remain in their homes.

The Plains Saloon was across the road with an abandoned beer wagon directly in front of it. The heavy wagon had stuck in the mud of the road, and the driver, after unloading some of the beer barrels and stacking them on the walk in front of the saloon, had given it up as a bad job, cut his harness horses out of the traces and left the wagon there until the weather cleared.

The beer wagon was in an ideal position if he wanted to look into the saloon without being seen. Cass pulled up at the edge of the boardwalk, looked up and down the deserted street for a moment, and then crossed hurriedly to the wagon, pulling himself up on the flat bed. He slipped in under the iron chains strung between the uprights, holding the beer barrels in place, and then he wriggled in between the barrels, working his way to the other side of the wagon. In starting to unload, the teamsters had left the heavy barrels scattered all over the wagon.

Lying on the wagon bed with the rain still

beating down on him, Cass pushed two of the barrels aside and looked through the opening. He was directly off the boardwalk here with the wooden awning just a few feet above him. From this position he could look over the bat-wing doors of the saloon and see the patrons at the bar.

The Plains Saloon was crowded in comparison with the others. The bar was half-filled, and he recognized several Slash M men there. He didn't see Munson or Bream. Several card games were going on inside the big room. A drunk came out of the door, walked to the edge of the boardwalk and held up his hand to see if it were still raining. The water was pouring off the awning roof in steady rivulets. The drunk was about three feet from Cass who was crouched on the beer wagon. He turned around, having satisfied himself, and walked back through the bat-wing doors.

Cass saw the door to the back room open and Ira Bream come out. It meant that Munson was back in there. Bream came out to the bar, paused to say a few words to another Slash M man, and then had a drink. As the Slash M ramrod stood at the bar, Cass could have easily have put a bullet through him. He crouched there, staring at Bream through the space between the beer barrels, the bitterness riding him hard now. This was the man who had put a bullet through Jeff with his wife and girl inside the house, and Jeff defenseless.

The man Bream had spoken to buttoned his slicker and went out into the night. Cass heard his boots sounding down the walk. Then he distinctly felt the beer wagon give a little as if someone had climbed up onto it. The lurch came from the rear end.

Quietly, Cass slipped his hand inside the slicker and came out with the gun. He held it close to his body, protecting the gun from the rain, and he waited, leaning on one side. He could hear someone crawling across the floor of the wagon, sliding in and out among the scattered beer barrels. Then the man stopped on the other side of a few barrels between himself and Cass. He was on Cass's side of the wagon now, facing the saloon, looking in through the doors. Cass could see his boots sprawled out a few inches beyond the barrels. He thought he could hear the man breathing.

His gun lined on the barrel which separated himself from the second man, Cass waited, wondering who this man was, and what he intended to do. A man who would crouch out here in the rain needed a pretty good reason to do so.

Ira Bream was chatting with the bartender inside as he sipped his drink, alone at the bar for the moment, the gunbelt sagging at his heavy waist, one hand shoved in his back pocket.

The man on the other side of the barrels shifted his position a little. Cass saw his boots move, and then he knew who the man was, and he wondered that he had not thought of it before.

Very slowly, he came up to a sitting position, and then a kneeling position, the gun still in his hand. He started to rise, hoping his joints wouldn't crack as he did so and give him away.

Still crouching, he leaned his weight over the barrel in front of him, sliding the muzzle of it down ahead of him. Then he said softly, "Still shooting from the brush, Arch?"

Young Arch Cummings spun around, his teeth drawn back in a snarl, face wet with rain, the water dripping from his chin. He still had his gun inside his slicker, and there was no time to go for it. The fear came into his eyes as he looked up into the muzzle of Cass's gun.

"You gunning for me or for Munson, Arch?"

"Munson," he scowled.

Cass nodded. "When you come after me," he said slowly, "come from the front, and come shooting."

Cummings didn't say anything. He lay there on the wagon bed, resting on one elbow, staring up at Cass.

Cass said to him, "Another thing, Arch. Don't touch Bream."

Arch Cummings lifted his eyebrows a little. "No?" he said gruffly.

"He's mine," Cass told him. "Understand that?"

"Got nothin' against Bream," Cummings growled.

Cass nodded. "Keep it in mind," he said. "Now get off and get your own wagon."

Arch Cummings didn't waste any time. Scrambling to his feet, he moved to the rear of the wagon and dropped down into the mud of the road. Cass lost sight of him as he swung around the corner of the building and darted into an alley. He squatted down behind the barrels again, not too pleased with the situation now. He knew where Ira Bream was, but Arch Cummings, who hated him, knew where he was, and young Arch would undoubtedly tip off the Slash M riders in a matter of moments.

Before Cass could get off the wagon something else happened. More riders were coming up, sloshing through the mud of Main Street, approaching the Plains Saloon. They dismounted in front of the tie rack a few yards from the abandoned wagon, and Cass saw them clearly in the light from the saloon. There were three of them—Matt Quinn, Morse Claybank and another of the homesteaders Cass had seen at Claybank's place.

They ducked under the tie rack and walked into the Plains Saloon, Quinn in the lead. Cass waited now, anxious to see this. Quinn walked straight up to Bream, Claybank behind him, and he had a few words with the Slash M ramrod.

Bream was shaking his head, smiling, trying to make light of the situation. Evidently, Claybank and the nesters had reached Matt Quinn and told him the story of the attempted raid on the house. Quinn was here now to arrest any of the men he could find who'd been in on the raid.

Cass saw one of them sitting in at a card game across the room. He didn't know the rider's name, but he was positive the man had been out to Claybank's place that morning.

Ira Bream went into the back room and came out a few moments later with Munson. Griff was smoking a cigar, smiling as usual. He spoke to Quinn at the bar, and it was then that Claybank spotted the Slash M rider at the card table.

The homesteader became quite excited. Matt Quinn left Munson and Bream and walked over to the table. Munson followed leisurely, and then Cass saw him turn his head and look at Bream significantly.

Bream downed the drink he'd left on the bar, wiped his lips, and then strolled into the back room. Cass watched the door close behind him, and he knew where Bream was going and what he intended to do. Matt Quinn had thrown in with the homesteaders which made him an enemy of Slash M. Quinn had to be stopped very abruptly.

The Slash M rider in the card game started to protest, but he shut up when Munson spoke to him. Cass saw him get up, and then Matt Quinn reached forward and took away his gun. This was to be an arrest with Quinn walking the Slash M man down to the jailhouse. On the way Quinn would stop a bullet from Ira Bream's gun—a bullet from an alley. Bream at this moment would be slipping out a back door or window, making his way through the back lots, locating the particular alley in which he would lie in wait for his prey.

As Quinn started toward the door, the Slash M rider ahead of him, Cass wriggled his way back across the wagon bed and dropped into the mud. He crossed the street, went up on the boardwalk, and hurried north in the direction of the jailhouse.

A block from the Plains Saloon he recrossed the road and entered an alley between the Empire Dry Goods Store and a warehouse. The jailhouse was another half block north, and this was the alley down which Bream would come.

Racing up the alley, Cass could hear the rain beating on empty tin cans, splattering into puddles. Already, Bream would be very close to this alley, threading his way through the vacant lots behind Main Street.

Cass Lorimer slipped the Colt gun from the holster, his heart beginning to pound now. He could feel the pressure on his temples, and he remembered all the nights he'd thought about this moment, wondering how it would be. He hadn't visualized that the affair would end in a pouring rain at the end of a dark alley in Red Rock.

He was still running quite hard when he reached the far end of the alley. He couldn't see at all down here, and he wanted to see his man when he shot him down. At the rear of the houses along Main Street there were occasional lights shining through the window, providing some small light. He wanted to be out here when Bream came up. He wanted to see the man's face, and he wanted Bream to see his face, and to know.

As he swung around the head of the alley he didn't expect Bream to be so close. The Slash M man had had plenty of time to get down here. He didn't expect Bream to be here and he didn't expect Bream to be running, but he was.

They met head-on, and Cass, who was the lighter man, staggered back from the impact, nearly losing his grip on the gun. His hat was almost shaken from his head as he fell back into a patch of light from a window in the rear of the Empire Dry Goods Store.

Ira Bream was at the edge of the patch of light about four feet away as Cass righted himself. There was a look on Bream's wide face which Cass Lorimer had never before seen on the face of a man. Bream was staring at him, his features frozen in terror. He started to point a finger, and his lips worked a moment before the words came out.

It was the dim light, the rain slanting down between them, distorting everything, and then there was the resemblance Cass bore to Jeff, not pronounced, but a resemblance.

Ira Bream whispered, "Jeff—Jeff Lorimer!"

Cass smiled grimly. He noticed that Bream already had his gun in his hand, ready to use it on Quinn when the sheriff passed the mouth of the alley. Waiting for several long, cruel seconds so that Bream would suffer the full measure of it, Cass said softly, "Not Jeff, Bream."

Bream knew, then, and a kind of sheepish smile crept across his face as he whipped up the heavy six-gun. Cass's bullet tore through his middle just as his gun went off. The bullet ripped through Cass's slicker close to the left leg.

Bream staggered back from the impact of the heavy caliber slug. He sat down in the mud, his face slack, and he started to shake his head like a big dog out in the rain. He died that way—still sitting up, and Cass walked around him, heading back toward the Plains Saloon.

When he looked back once he noticed that Bream's body had fallen back, and the rain was beating into his face now. He walked without haste, knowing that the shots had been heard. In a very short while they would find Bream's body, and they would know who had killed him.

Griff Munson was still in the Plains Saloon,

though, and Munson was the man who'd sent Bream. Munson had to pay too.

There was a loading platform at the rear of the saloon. Several empty beer barrels stood on the platform, and the door beyond was ajar. Bream had come out through that door a few minutes before for his last walk in the rain.

Cass hoisted himself up on the platform, stepped to the door, and pushed it open. He had the gun ready now, and he waited, listening. This was a storeroom, dark, damp, half-filled with beer barrels. The tang of stale beer assailed his nostrils as he stepped inside. He thought he heard a rat scurrying away in a dark corner.

There was a crack of light across the room where the door to the main building opened up. Cass crossed the storeroom, felt around for the doorknob, and then opened the door slowly. He came into a dimly-lit corridor, and he could hear the noise from the main saloon dead ahead.

There were several doors off the corridor. He tried one of them. It was locked. The second one opened into the room in which he'd met Munson on two different occasions. Munson had been playing solitaire when Bream came in to call him. The cards were still laid out on the table.

The room was empty as Cass looked in. He stepped in, started to walk softly across it toward the door leading into the saloon when he felt the muzzle of a gun jammed into the small of his back.

Griff Munson said to him softly, "Reckon you walked far enough, Lorimer. Drop the gun."

Cass stiffened. He stood there, the water dripping from his slicker and from his hat, calculating his chances now. Munson had undoubtedly heard him at the door and he'd stepped behind it when Cass pushed it open, thinking the room was empty.

Munson, as if reading his thoughts, said easily, "I'll blow a hole through you, Lorimer, if you make a move. Drop that gun."

Cass dropped it, cursing himself inwardly for his carelessness. He said over his shoulder, "Blow a hole through me, Munson, and Matt Quinn will be on your neck."

"Quinn's taken care of," Munson chuckled.

Fighting for time, Cass said softly, "Is he?"

That had Griff Munson guessing for the moment. He'd heard the shots up the street, and he'd naturally assumed that Ira Bream had done for Quinn.

Cass said, "Take a look outside, Munson. You might find Quinn coming through the door—looking for the man who shot up Bream."

Griff Munson walked around him and kicked his gun into a corner. The big man's face was tight and hard, his turquoise eyes gleaming in the lamplight. He said slowly, "So you got Bream,

Lorimer. That's what you came for, wasn't it?"

Cass nodded. "Didn't get you, yet," he stated. "I will."

Munson backed to the door leading to the saloon. He stood there, his six-gun lined on Cass's chest eight feet away, the gun hand very steady.

"You will?" Munson repeated softly. "You crossed my trail once too often tonight, mister."

Outside, Cass could hear the rain beating against the windows. A small pool of water formed on the floor around him. He looked straight at Munson, wondering if the boss of Slash M would dare put a bullet in him here, or have him taken out in the back. He thought the latter. In the past Griff Munson had always preferred his dead men to be murdered anonymously.

Munson had his left hand on the doorknob. He looked at Cass as if warning him not to make a move, and then he opened the door a crack. He said to Cass, "Step back to the far wall, Lorimer."

Cass started to move back. Munson wanted to call one or two of his riders in, and he didn't want Cass too close when he turned his head for the fraction of a second.

Backing to the wall, Cass waited, wondering if he could leap through the open door to the corridor during that fraction of a second Munson took his eyes off him to look into the saloon. It was a long chance, but it was a chance. The door was about ten feet to his right. He didn't dare look that way, knowing that Munson would read his thoughts. He kept his eyes on Munson's face, and then that small hope died in him.

Munson wasn't turning his head. Smiling, the gun steady in his grasp, his eyes fixed on Cass, Munson called sharply, "George—George Hemsley."

That was when the gun sounded from the corridor door. It boomed three times, and each time Griff Munson's body seemed to be rammed hard with an invisible pole. One bullet took him in the stomach, and he dropped his hands to the place, his face contorted as he started to spin.

He staggered forward a few steps, coming toward Cass, looking at him, the hell in his eyes. The gun banged again—the fourth time—this bullet striking him in the temple. He pitched forward on his face, his body hitting the floor with a heavy thud which shook the room.

Cass caught a glimpse of Arch Cummings' hate-filled face just outside the doorway from the corridor. He was already moving when Arch fired the last shot at Munson, knowing that Arch's gun would be coming at himself next.

He made a long headlong dive for Munson's gun, his own being too far away. Even then he was too late. Cummings' first bullet hammered into the baseboard an inch from his head as he lay on the floor, his fingers closing around the pearl handle of the gun. He didn't have time to swing around and line his gun on Cummings. It was too late—much too late. He had one big regret—that a cheap, cowardly bushwhacker like Arch Cummings should be the man to kill him.

The final shot never came from Cummings' gun. Another shot rang from the corridor behind Cummings, and young Arch stumbled into the room, his eyes glassy. He was sagging, the gun drooping in his hand. He looked around drunkenly, trying to find Cass, to put that last bullet into him, but he couldn't focus his eyes. He started to curse, then, the futile, hopeless oaths of a small boy. His legs gave way and he collapsed as if all the bones in his body were turned to jelly. He fell across Griff Munson.

Cass was sitting up, the gun in his hand, when Matt Quinn appeared in the doorway from the corridor. Quinn had a gun in his hand. He looked down at Cummings and at Munson, and then he grimaced. He said to Cass, "He shoot Bream too? I found Bream at the end of Paradise Alley, and I came back this way. Cummings, here, was sneaking in through the back door. I followed him."

"I shot Bream," Cass told him.

Sheriff Quinn looked at him, a frown coming to his face. "Still throwin' lead, Kincaid?" he asked.

"I threw it," Cass said quietly, "at the man who murdered my brother—Jeff Lorimer."

Matt Quinn lifted his eyebrows a little. He said simply, "Figured you weren't Ty Kincaid, mister. I knew Kincaid down in El Paso."

The door from the saloon opened and several Slash M men looked in. The black-haired George Hemsley, the man Cass had seen with Moran, was in the lead. They looked at Munson on the floor, and at Arch Cummings.

Cass was standing up now. He said to them, "Show's over, boys. Reckon you can move out."

Hemsley grinned. "Who killed who?" he asked curiously.

"Come around to the inquest," Matt Quinn told him.

When the Slash M men left, Cass said, "Munson has a sister out at the ranch, Quinn. Reckon you'll have to go around and see her."

Quinn nodded. "Bad business," he scowled, "but Munson had it coming to him. Claybank told me all about it—the way Munson was trying to get control of the creek and the gold deposits. I came in tonight to pick up the riders who'd come out to Claybank's place this morning, but I wasn't stopping them."

Cass slipped his gun into the holster. He said, "Reckon they're feeling pretty good up on the creek. Even if they don't make a fortune they should be able to take enough gold out of the creek bed to set them up decently."

Quinn was looking at him curiously. "Your job is finished here, Lorimer. What happens next?"

Cass shrugged. He started to button his slicker. "Cup of coffee waiting for me first, Sheriff."

Quinn rubbed his chin. "Yeah?"

"At Katie McCoy's," Cass added thoughtfully. He saw the relief come into Quinn's eyes. The sheriff of Red Rock smiled faintly.

"Reckon that's nice," he murmured.

"Tell Miss Schuyler I was asking about her," Cass said.

"I'll do that," Quinn nodded. He scratched his chin again. "You goin' out to Katie's now?" he asked.

"Now," Cass nodded.

"Rainin' like hell," Quinn observed.

Cass adjusted his hat. "Reckon I won't notice it, Sheriff," he said softly.

Cass Lorimer passed out through the saloon, moving between the groups of men who were looking at him curiously. Out on the porch he paused for a few moments to watch the rain, and then he stepped out into it and headed up toward the Ace High Livery. The rain felt good in his face now. It was a cold and a clean rain, and it made everything new and fresh again. He felt that way too. Cass Lorimer felt good.

Center Point Large Print
600 Brooks Road / PO Box 1
Thorndike, ME 04986-0001 USA

(207) 568-3717

**US & Canada:
1 800 929-9108**
www.centerpointlargeprint.com